P9-CLN-467

Withdrawn

ZOMBIE TAG

ZOMBIE TAG

Hannah Moskowitz

ROARING BROOK PRESS
New York

Published by Roaring Brook Press

Roaring Brook Press is a division of
Holtzbrinck Publishing Holdings Limited Partnership
175 Fifth Avenue, New York, New York 10010

mackids.com

Library of Congress Cataloging-in-Publication Data

Moskowitz, Hannah.
    Zombie Tag / Hannah Moskowitz. — 1st ed.
       p. cm.
    Summary: In the months since Wil Lowenstein's older brother Graham died,
Wil has spent most of his time playing a game he invented but when he finds a
way to bring Graham and others back from the dead, fighting zombies is
suddenly no longer a game.
    ISBN 978-1-59643-720-3 (alk. paper)
    [1. Zombies—Fiction. 2. Dead—Fiction. 3. Brothers—Fiction. 4. Tag
games—Fiction. 5. Grief—Fiction. 6. Supernatural—Fiction.] I. Title.

PZ7.M84947Zom 2011
[Fic]—dc22
                                                                    2010043940

Roaring Brook Press books are available for special promotions and premiums.
For details contact: Director of Special Markets, Holtzbrinck Publishers.

First edition 2011
Book design by Alex Garkusha
Printed in November 2011 in the United States of America
by RR Donnelley & Sons Company, Harrisonburg, Virginia

3 5 7 9 8 6 4 2

To Emma: the Wil to my Anthony

and

Abby: the Wil to my Graham

I ONLY INVENTED ZOMBIE TAG three weeks ago, and we've already lost seven spatulas. For a while, I stole my mom's, but now she's completely out so I have to make my friends bring their own. Once our mothers find out where all their spatulas are going, they're going to be so mad. They're going to team up and form some kind of army against us, I swear. But we'd be totally prepared. A mom army is nothing when you're trained to fight zombies.

Today is Anthony's birthday, so we should be sleeping over at his house. But Anthony has an awful house for Zombie Tag. His place is like a museum. There's all this great stuff, but you can't touch any of it. And there's nowhere to sit. My house still feels new and unfriendly, but, tonight, that's a bonus. It's fresh territory to explore.

But because it's his birthday, we let Anthony be

Zombie God. That means he's the one who writes the words on the Post-it Notes—BARRICADE, BARRICADE, BARRICADE, BARRICADE, ZOMBIE. It's pitch-black down here, so he's using his phone for light. David's using his to look up zombie fighting strategies, which is so dumb. I've read everything there is to read about zombies, and let me tell you, there are no little tricks for how to survive. It takes pure brute force. And courage.

And a really good spatula doesn't hurt.

The air-conditioning is on too high because my dad is always hot, and here in the basement it feels like the tundra. We're all jumping up and down and shivering while Anthony folds and shuffles the Post-it Notes.

Eben comes thumping down the stairs. "Dude, shut up," I say. "My parents are sleeping."

"All the lights are off," he says. He's panting from running through the entire house. He volunteered to do this, so he should man up and stop acting like he just ran a marathon or something.

Anthony clears his throat dramatically. "Okay," he says, holding the Post-it Notes above his head. "We will begin. No trading, no showing, no sharing." He passes them out. We peek at them and stuff the evidence into our pockets.

I can't believe it. I'm Zombie. In our millions of games of Zombie Tag, this is my first time being the Zombie. It's like it's *my* birthday.

But no one would know from my face. I am the world's coolest cucumber right now. They'll all think I'm innocent until the moment I'm chewing on their brains.

"Okay, eyes closed," our Zombie God orders. We snap our eyes closed, and I slowly open mine to make sure the others aren't peeking. They have their fingers stuffed into their ears, just like they're supposed to. I feel kind of proud that they're following my rules so well. It's not every guy who has a bunch of friends who really understand how sacred a thing like Zombie Tag is, you know? We've made up a lot of games over the years, especially me and Anthony, but ideas this good only come along once in a millennium. They're smart to recognize it.

Time to fulfill my first duty as Zombie. I walk away from the circle as quietly as I can. I put all my weight on my heels before I lean onto each toe. When I was a kid, my brother told me that hunters used to walk like this so they didn't get eaten by tigers. I totally believed him and put it in an early settlers history paper a few weeks ago, and Ms. Hoole gave me a C and wrote THERE

3

ARE NO TIGERS IN THE UNITED STATES. Like that was even the point.

I keep my tiger-sneak walk going until I'm well out of the circle, then I run to the table and pick up the dinosaur. It's this plastic coin bank my dad got me as a souvenir when he went to Russia with his boss to turn in all this paperwork on Time-Based Travel. He was all excited about going and kept telling mom that this was his big break but then he came home all depressed. I think the Russians are beating us at time travel or something.

Anyway, he had this whole stack of papers to work through and all these reports to file, like everyone on the trip gave their busy work to him. I asked if he was a spy just so he'd feel less lame, but then he said, "Quiet, Wil," and that's when he gave me this bank. And, it's like, I'm not six, Dad, but at least it comes in useful for Zombie Tag.

It's our Key. The other guys need to find the Key and then get to the front door in order to win. But that's not going to happen. Sorry, guys. And if they don't find the Key, I get to eat their brains.

I mean, they can try to defend themselves with the spatulas, but I'm going to be the scariest Zombie ever. They'd need, like, three spatulas each at least to fight me off.

I run upstairs and look for a good place to hide the Key. My parents' room is totally out. If they knew we were still awake, they'd probably start putting tranquilizers in our food every time my friends stay over. It's a good thing they're heavy sleepers. Graham and I used to watch horror movies after they went to bed, and they'd hardly ever wake up.

I can't do my room. Too easy.

I pause outside of the extra bedroom we don't even use as a guest room. My friends aren't allowed to sleep in there when they stay over. We all have to crash in the basement.

I'm pretty sure I'm not even supposed to go in there, because every time my dad or I step inside, Mom spends an hour fluffing the pillows and vacuuming over where we stepped. My mother set up all the baseball trophies and put my brother's framed posters of girls in bathing suits, the ones she always hated, up on one of the walls. The room's made up like any minute he's going to come home and need it.

Dad tells me not to think about it. We had to put my brother's stuff somewhere. It's just a place.

I know Dad's right, but I'm looking in there now and don't want my friends tramping around in there, either. I guess Mom has brainwashed me.

So I hide the Key in the bathroom, behind the clothes hamper. It's not the best spot, but it'll still be hard to find in the dark and I'm running out of time to find anywhere better. There's no rule for how long you can take to hide the Key, but it's lame to be this slow.

I turn off my flashlight and scurry back downstairs. I run around the circle and tap each guy on the back, so they'll know the Key has been hidden. I give Anthony a squeeze on the back of his neck just to scare him. They count to ten in their heads, and I'm back in the circle before their eyes are open. I blink stupidly and look around just like them. They have no idea I'm the Zombie, and it's awesome.

"Okay," David says. "I'll take the downstairs."

I say, "I'll look with you." He's totally going to be my first victim. Poor David. So young.

We grab our spatulas, fighting over the best ones, but not for very long. We have to hurry up and separate. The fewer guys you're with, the less chance you're with the Zombie.

The other guys go upstairs to look for the Key. David switches on his flashlight and starts poking around behind the boxes we still haven't unpacked. I pretend to search too, but really I'm counting to ten. Zombies have a ten-second lifespan as humans. Then they can start their hunt.

Once I've gotten to ten, I flop down on the floor, as quietly as I can. I try to pretend I'm just looking under the couch. Really, I'm dying.

My favorite part of this game is the dying, because I'm screwed up, I guess. I always liked the part where Bambi's mom died, too. Now I think it's awful, but when I was a little kid, I made my mom play it again and again. Maybe the most messed up part is that she did.

I've almost finished my ten seconds of dying when David says, "Dude, find anything?"

I stand up and go, "Rrrrrrrn. Braaaains."

"Ah! No way, Wil!"

"Braaaaaaaains."

"You're the Zombie?"

He takes too long to try to run, and I grab him and hold him by the neck. He's flailing around, trying to hit me with his spatula. If he hits the top of my head, I'll have to freeze. But he doesn't make it. I try to sink my teeth into his ear.

He shrieks.

"Shh!" I say. "Count to ten."

"You're breaking character."

"Shut up and count to ten."

He squeezes his eyes shut and counts to ten. He has his death perfected; he always grips his chest and shakes like his insides are trying to get out. When he opens his eyes, he has the perfect practiced zombie look on his face. David has been the Zombie so many times. It's not fair at all.

"Neeeeeeeeed braaaaaaaaains," he groans.

I nod toward the stairs, and we start marching there together, our arms out. "Braaaaains," we chant.

We search around the hallway with our flashlights. Anthony and Stella are rooting through my bedroom. They left the door open, which was so stupid of them. If they closed the door and put one of their BARRICADE Post-its on it, we'd have to bang our zombie fists against it for a whole thirty seconds before we could come in. Now we can just walk right in and turn them into the undead.

But scaring them first is way more fun.

David and I spy from the doorway. Stella found one of my secret magazines, and she's looking at it with her flashlight and laughing. "Anthony, you have to see this. There are naked girls in here!"

I am so going to eat her brains.

I jump out and go, "Rrrrrn!" and Stella and Anthony scream so loudly that my cat Jack Bandit sprints into the closet with his fur standing up.

Anthony tries to fight us off with his spatula. Stella tries to bop me on top of my head for the secret zombie paralysis move. But it's no use. We're too fast, and we bob away from their hands like it's nothing.

I grab Anthony, David grabs Stella, and we bite down. Those guys are zombie-toast.

Anthony takes his ten seconds to recover, then says, "Brains."

I nod at him. "Braaains."

We go into the hallway. Here's the big problem. There's only Eben left, and if he finds the Key and gets to the front door, he escapes with his brains intact. And judging by the closed bathroom door with the BARRICADE sign on the door, he might have a chance. And there's no way I'm letting *Eben* win Zombie Tag in my house.

"Break barricade need brains want," Anthony drones, and he starts banging on the door. We all join in. Eben's totally freaking out in there. We can hear him scurrying around and mumbling, "Oh God oh God oh God oh God."

I'm banging on the door as hard as I can.

I guess it's from being up so late, but I start having a harder time focusing on the game every second I'm pounding. I hate when this happens, and it still does way too often, even if it's not as often as it was.

In most ways I'm doing better. I don't have nightmares anymore. But I'll be doing something totally normal, like taking a test or trying to fall asleep, and my brain will start freaking out and telling me that I have to go save Graham. And I'm telling myself *stop it, stop being so stupid,* but I can't shake the feeling. Every bit of me needs to get to Graham now, and I can do it, I can save him if I just *do something*.

I don't know anything in the whole world except that I have to get into that bathroom right now. I'm banging on it and the noise is echoing in my ears a million times.

"Stop screaming," Anthony says, and I wish whoever's screaming *would* stop screaming. Then Anthony clamps his hand over my mouth and the screaming gets softer. It's me. I'm the one screaming. I can still hear it in my head, even though I think I've stopped.

And Anthony broke character.

There are footsteps behind me, and I hear my father's voice, always so low and scratchy, like he needs to shave the inside of his throat. "What *time* do you guys think it is? WIL!"

But I don't care that he's mad. I have to get into that bathroom. This isn't a game anymore.

They have to let me into the bathroom now. I can get in and . . .

No.

I'm coming back to real life. No. I'm so stupid. I'll get in and no one will be there but stupid old Eben.

Stella goes, "Sorry, Mr. Lowenstein." She doesn't sound nervous. She's so used to getting in trouble. "Eben, come out, man. Game's over."

The bathroom door opens, and my chest is like *whunka whunka whunka*, but it's just Eben. I knew that. I knew it was just going to be Eben.

I shake my head back and forth. I need to spend more time in real life. Maybe I should watch less TV.

Or lose fewer brothers.

"Downstairs," my father says. "Back downstairs. Wilson, we're going to be discussing this in the morning."

I wish he wouldn't do this in front of my friends. But I guess after I have some sort of mental breakdown in front of them, I shouldn't be embarrassed about getting lectured.

"Okay, Dad," I mumble. And before he goes back to bed, I give him a hug. My friends probably think I'm sucking up, but I just want someone to hold me up for a second. He does. At least I know he's not too mad.

We slump back downstairs. We don't know if the zombies beat Eben, which sucks. So far, every time we've played, the zombies have won. I bet we would have won this time, too.

Anthony whispers to me, "Was that about Graham?"

I crawl into my sleeping bag and say, "Shut up."

Everyone else falls asleep, but I stay awake and make up this story to myself about the zombies winning and nobody has any brains and nobody's thinking anymore, and everything is always fun. And I *always* make it into the bathroom in time. And then I bite my brother and he screams and comes back to life.

What's funny about my brother Graham dying is that he was one of the most alive people I ever knew. He was always running around and slamming doors and screaming at my parents or cutting his hair off or lifting me onto his shoulders or tackling me onto the rug. It's also funny because he always fought so hard to stay that way.

"Let's never grow up," he said to me one time. I must have been about seven.

I said, "Okay," because I didn't get it, but I liked to do everything Graham did.

We spit on our hands and shook them to seal the deal, and he said, "Good. We're going to be exactly like this forever. You and me, kid."

And I said, "Me and you, kid," which made him smile so much, and I felt really good about that.

THE NEXT MORNING at breakfast, my parents drag the whole story of Zombie Tag out of me. We've been playing it constantly for weeks, but they're acting like I've been keeping it some big secret. But I guess I didn't want them to find out, because I knew I'd get these concerned looks and this lecture about how zombies are very serious and not something I should joke about, and do I really want to be the kind of kid who makes games out of serious things?

"What's next?" my father says. "Anemia Tag? Endangered Species Tag?"

I say, "It's just a game, Dad. It's fun to bite people and talk about brains and stuff."

My mother watches me, shaking her head slowly while she bites her lip. I feel like I'm a very sad book she's reading, or a kid in one of her classes who answered a question really, really wrong.

Dad says, "You know, Anthony's father spends hours in the office—away from his family, Wil—trying to make sure that game of yours doesn't become a reality."

I wish my dad had a job that cool. Mr. Lohen is this big-time public official who's on the news all the time talking about our personal safety and the discoveries he's made and the treaties he's written. He's always talking in this soothing voice and reassuring the public that we don't need to be worried about whatever people are worried about this week. Then he shakes hands with the president and signs all these important documents while people take pictures.

Mr. Lohen gets to meet all these creatures the rest of us aren't even sure exist. Anthony swears his dad touched a unicorn once, when he was in Greenland visiting the prime minister. It's weird how much Anthony brags about his dad since he doesn't even like him. Meanwhile, I like my dad a lot but he doesn't give me anything to brag about, because all he does is file papers about Time-Based Travel, which isn't even going to be real for years and years. The people who will use it won't know that he worked on it. Sometimes I think there's nothing in the whole world as stupid as having a job. At least Mr. Lohen gets to do his on TV.

Mom keeps touching my hands. "Wil. Honey." Then she can't decide what she wants to say. She's stuck between all these different speeches. *Do I give him the "We should go back to the doctor with the soothing voice" speech or the "You should eat less red meat" speech or the "Dead people don't come back" speech?*

Ever since six months ago, when my older brother Graham died in the bathroom looking for his inhaler, my mom's been kind of in charge of making sure none of us gets on with our life too well. Just when we think we're doing okay, she mentions his name with a wistful sigh or whispers about how dinner would taste so much better if there were four of us here to eat it. But it's actually nice sometimes, because otherwise we just sit around the table and scrape at our plates, waiting for someone else to talk. And then Dad gets up to leave, making that smile that he thinks hides how crumpled and shaky his face is, and Mom and I scrape at our plates and pretend we're alone. It's no wonder they let my friends sleep over here all the time, because we just need someone else to look at. We get really sick of each other's faces.

"I'm okay," I tell my mom. "It's just a game. We got too loud. It doesn't mean anything."

Mom keeps watching me.

She hasn't been the same since it happened. She's always getting paralyzed by small things, like I ask her to take me to a friend's house and she just sits there and stares at me, or she tries to put on a pair of socks and has to sit with them in her hand for hours before she figures out how to go on.

But Dad's worse than Mom, to be honest. He used to take me and Graham out to see monster trucks all the time, which I always thought were stupid, but Graham was really into them. He and his best friend Luke—Anthony's brother—used to trade programs from the shows and talk about statistics and miles per hour. Luke has all these posters of his favorite cars in his room. Sometimes now he lets me come in to look at them, and we talk about the races and stuff. I research some facts before I go over, so I'll have something to tell him and he'll be impressed and let me stay, even though then Anthony gets mad I'm not hanging out with him. But sometimes when I'm in Luke's room long enough, he'll stop talking about monster trucks and start talking about Graham.

Luke and Graham weren't really much alike, which made them weird friends, because Luke is calmer and happier, but if I make him talk about Graham long enough he gets upset and touchy and angry. And that reminds me of Graham, so I always end up pushing him there.

Anyway, ever since Graham died, Dad doesn't take me to see monster trucks anymore, like it was only worth the time off work when he had two sons. I'm not as much fun as Graham, maybe. He was sixteen, so he and Dad could have all these conversations that were way too boring for me to follow, so now I don't know how to imitate them. But since Dad and I don't hang out, I guess it doesn't really matter.

The truth is, I miss Graham, but sometimes I miss Mom and Dad more.

"Wil," Mom says, when she's finally decided on a speech. "I know it's been a hard year. But daydreaming about *zombies* isn't something a boy your age should be doing with his free time."

I say, "Anthony says no one even cares about zombies because they're not going to be real again ever. His dad says no way, no more zombies."

"Why have you been discussing this with Anthony?"

Dad says, and that's when I realize I said "real again." A good kid would pretend he never thinks about when there were zombies. A good kid probably wouldn't have spent hours on the Internet reading about them. I'm digging myself deeper and deeper. I need a lawyer right now.

I just roll my eyes and say, "I can read, you know."

Dad says, "Wil, what have we told you about getting involved?"

"Getting involved" is Dad's slang for thinking ahead past what I'm going to have for breakfast tomorrow.

"Everyone knows there were zombies," I say. "They told us in school."

Dad's still looking at me really suspiciously, probably because he knows they didn't tell us in school.

The details from the last zombie observation are completely top secret. This is stupid, but right now the main reason I wish I knew the details is so I could throw it in Dad's face that I know and he doesn't.

But I don't. I know what's on the Internet, which is basically nothing. Zombie Tag didn't come from too much research; it came from my messed-up head. But saying that would probably freak them out even more.

I say, "I'm not like a government menace or something, okay? We were playing tag."

"It's a dangerous line of thinking," Dad says. "Wondering if dead people are going to come back. You'll get yourself into trouble." And that's all he has time to say to me, because he has so much work to do. He gets up and leaves. His jacket is all crumpled in the back, like someone grabbed him by it.

Mom takes my hand across the table. "We're worried about you."

I nod, but I know that's not the right response. My brain is going really fast. Something just happened.

Because she and Dad are worried about me, yeah, but my well-being isn't what they're concerned about right now. They're not scared I need to go back to therapy. They're scared I'm poking around somewhere I shouldn't be. I know it.

But before I can drag any information out of her, Mom says she has to get something out of the oven. I make a face because it smells like dead cabbage, and she rolls her eyes and tells me I can go hang out at Anthony's.

"Do you ever get frustrated?" Graham asked me once, about a year ago. We were sitting outside the garage watching Dad work on his car, and Graham was drawing him. He was a really good artist, and he always said he would teach me how to draw someday.

I said, "Frustrated?"

"Yeah." He kept his voice all quiet like he didn't want Dad to hear.

"I don't know."

"It's just . . ." He looked down at his paper. "Like, why am I drawing this? What's it for? It's not like it's ever going to hang in a museum. And even if it did, what would that prove? That some people who don't know me are willing to pay a few dollars to look at this picture of Dad and a car and wonder what it's about?"

"It's good," I told him. "I like the steering wheel."

"But what's the point of being good?"

I liked that he talked to me, but I hated that he expected me to have something to say back. "Um . . . I don't know."

He put the picture down and crouched next to me. "What are you doing?"

"Fixing the wagon." Its wheel kept sliding off of the axle, so Dad gave me his tool kit because I said I wanted to try to fix it myself. I had no idea what I was doing, besides probably making it worse.

But then here was Graham, looking at me like I was the smartest person he'd ever seen. It felt like my insides grew a little bigger.

"Can I help?" he asked after a minute.

"Yeah."

He sat down next to me. He wasn't any help at all. But he tried all the things I'd already tried and handed me tools when I asked for them. We tested wrenches and screwdrivers by tapping them against the wagon's red side and making up scientific talk about their strength and accuracy and what make and model they were.

"This is awesome," I said. I didn't care that we weren't getting anything done, I was just happy that Graham wasn't yelling at me.

"So then what?" he said. "After we finish this? Then what happens?"

"I don't know. We can put water balloons in here and wheel them over to the Lohens' and throw them at Luke and Anthony when they aren't paying attention. We can do anything we want with it."

"You don't want to decide ahead of time?"

I said, "Why?"

He was quiet for a while, and I felt like I'd said something wrong.

So I said, "We can do whatever we want. It's okay." What I meant was, *we can do whatever you want, Graham,* but I didn't say that out loud.

Then he mumbled, "Never change," and moved to get a better look at the axle. His drawing got crushed underneath his sneaker when he scooted over, but I don't think he cared.

We never fixed the wagon. And that was okay. We just played with something else instead.

I DIDN'T MEAN TO start researching zombies. Right after Graham died, I was pretty much okay. I fell apart in a tidy way. I cried at the funeral and slacked off on homework for a few weeks, but I never unglued myself from reality like Mom and Dad did.

Then I started getting weird. I stopped closing the bathroom door when I was in there, which was kind of bizarre. And I had to know where everyone was all the time. I got antsy if my parents left the room, and I started begging to stay home from school every day, but whenever I did stay home, I'd get freaked out about all my friends at school and worry that they were sick or something. It wasn't cool.

So after that, after I went as totally bananas as I ever did, I started doing research on bringing dead people back to life.

The truth is, I know way more about zombies than anyone would like me to. I even know how I'd go about bringing Graham back, if I were going to do it. There's this thing, basically an alarm clock for dead people, but the Internet says no one has any idea where it is. It's probably buried in some cave and booby-trapped and explosive and covered in guns or something. And even though everyone knows there were zombies thirty years ago, no one saw them and no one has any idea what they were like or why they all dropped dead again before anyone ever saw them awake. When a kid at school begged Ms. Hoole to talk about them, she made a big point of reminding us that it was just a theory, that nobody can say for sure that they were really zombies. Yeah. They were just a bunch of people who were supposed to have already been dead, discovered aboveground miles away, dead again. Just a theory, sure.

The main point is that there are zero, absolutely zero, real reports of what the real zombies were like, so there's a good chance that if I brought Graham back, he'd be just as brain-hungry as I was last night.

Finding all that out for the first time really freaked me out. I updated my anti-zombie weapons just in case. I made sure I had a baseball bat put away, a can of bug spray, and a few of the really good spatulas. Just in case.

Nothing online gave me any reason to believe the real zombies weren't just like the ones from the movies Graham and I used to watch, so I don't know why the techniques we figured out wouldn't really work. That's what Zombie Tag is, really. It's practicing all the methods Graham and I discovered. It's training.

And I can't tell my Dad without him wanting to arrest me, and it's probably never going to matter because Anthony says there's no way the zombies are coming back. His dad would know, he says.

I get off the bus and start the three-block walk to Anthony's house. We grew up with the Lohens next door, and even now that we've moved, it's like Mom forgets they're not still a few steps away. I'm not allowed to bike to the store by myself, but I'm allowed to take two different buses across town to get to Anthony's all on my own. She gives me the money to do it. It's really stupid, but I'm not complaining.

The cemetery where Graham's buried is on this first block. I walk past it every time I come. Sometimes I stop by the grave, but it never makes me feel much of anything. I don't go in today, but I wave, like always.

When I get to Anthony's, Eben's already there. Eben's a year younger than us, which is the difference between going into seventh grade and going into sixth grade. And there's a huge difference between a kid who's been through a year of middle school and a kid who has no idea what he's in for. Eben keeps asking us all about it, too, which is kind of like asking what the zombie takeover's going to be like. You can only know when you're there.

Anthony hangs out with Eben because he lives next door now. We knew him kind of casually through swim team, and then when his family heard we were moving, they parked themselves in my old house. Now, Eben's always trying to invite me in to show me how he's set up his room—*my* room. He says he has a big-screen TV in there that he got for Hanukkah. I got socks for Hanukkah.

When I let myself in through Anthony's front door, he and Eben have the refrigerator and all the cabinets open, and they're cramming stuff into the blender. I bet they're going to forget the top before they turn it on. It's going to be like every TV show episode ever.

"Yo, son," Eben says, which is how he always says hello. I really don't get it.

I say, "Hey."

"We're making coffee smoothies," Anthony tells me. "Want one?"

"What?"

27

"Smoothies with coffee beans in them," Eben says. "It's really hardcore."

"I'm totally overwhelmed by your bravery," with a big eye roll so he knows I don't mean it.

But he ignores me. "We should put raw egg in it."

Anthony's eyes get enormous. "That's *toxic*."

"The guys in the Olympics do it."

I say, "I saw this woman on the news who ate raw egg, and she was in the hospital for like three weeks. She almost lost a leg." I'm making this up, but I have a good lying face, and Anthony gives me this nod that says he appreciates it. But I think he's being a little drippy, to be honest. What kind of guy is afraid of an egg?

Anthony's always been pretty drippy, and I say this as his best friend. It's annoying, but I'm used to him. And after Graham died, it was nice, because I was pretty drippy myself, and Anthony and I could freak out together about what if someone broke into our lockers or what if we got lost on the way home from school. But now I'm pretty much okay, and he's still always trying to get me to talk about how I'm feeling, which is kind of messed up. It's not a big secret. I'm feeling like I wish my brother were back.

I say, "Put the top on the blender," and Eben rolls

his eyes but listens. They blend everything up, but the ground-up coffee beans stay sludged at the bottom. I'm totally not drinking this.

"So did you get reamed?" Anthony asks while he drinks. He's trying not to gag.

I say, "Yeah. My parents are really anti-Zombie Tag. They'd rather I did something safe and normal like juggle chainsaws or shoot at pigeons."

Eben looks like he'd totally be up for either of those. Little freak.

Anthony says, "If my dad found out about Zombie Tag, he'd be so pissed," and I feel a little bad. I know I'm glossing over my dad's issues with the situation, but it's not like I'm going to talk about this seriously in front of *Eben*.

"It's not even that fun," Eben says, which is so stupid, because he totally loves Zombie Tag, and he's the one who's always begging to play it every time we get together. Even when it's light outside, and that's just dumb.

I sit down at the bar and watch them try to choke down the smoothies. I feel all old and wise now. I say, "I'm pretty sure the only thing cooler than Zombie Tag is actual zombies. Actually."

Anthony says, "Dude, shut up. My dad's home. If he hears . . ."

He's such a drip. He's dripping all over the place. I say, "Why can't I say zombies are cool? Can I say *dragons* are cool?"

Eben snorts. "You're still into *dragons*?"

I have a stuffed dragon hidden under my bed, but that's totally not the point.

Anthony says, "My dad met a dragon once."

Eben raises his eyebrows. "Dude, he did not." Eben thinks his dad is the only one who can do anything cool, just because he's at the South Pole hunting yetis. Yeah, it sounds cool, but I Googled them and found out they're just hairy cows. Lame.

"He totally did," Anthony says. "In Alaska when he was a kid."

Eben narrows his eyes. "Dragons don't live in Alaska, dude. Dragons live where it's *hot*."

"Idiot, if it was hot, no one would notice when they lit stuff on fire."

I say, "There aren't any dragons and there aren't any zombies. Anymore. So why do I have to be quiet about them? They're going to find me and eat me if I talk about them? They're *not here*. Zombies, zombies, zombies." I stand up and do some of the karate David taught me while I chant something I'm making up that sounds sort of like Latin. "I'm summoning the zombies. Guba le duban vay sprockenze zombie."

Anthony says, "Wil, you are so stupid."

"I'm not stupid. I know all about zombies."

Eben's looking at me with these wide eyes. "Really?" I forgot that they won't tell you about zombies until sixth grade. Yet another thing he doesn't know. What an infant.

I make this big sigh like he's making me go through so much trouble, then I say, "The last time they woke up zombies was like thirty years ago, and no one even knew about it until they found them all dead in a heap miles away from where they were buried, and nobody even knows anything and that's the end of it."

"Boring," Eben says.

"Except they found this bell right next to them," I say. "And then the government took the bell . . ."

"Shhh!" Anthony leans forward and drops his voice into a dramatic whisper. "Listen. I know all about this bell. Trust me."

I raise my eyebrows. "Yeah?"

"It's called the Wake-Up bell." Anthony's so smug

31

when he thinks he's telling me something I don't know. He turns to Eben with this look on his face like we should both drop to our knees and worship him. Eben looks like he might. "And it brings back all the dead people within, like, a hundred miles."

It's *five* miles. Anthony should really get his stories peer-reviewed or something.

But Eben's like, "No way."

"Totally. And it's illegal to ring. Anyone who tries will get arrested. Do you want to get arrested, Wil?"

"Not really."

I don't know if it's illegal. I didn't read anything that said it wasn't. I don't know how it can be illegal when, according to the government, it doesn't officially exist.

"So there you go." He takes a defiant sip of his smoothie, but I can tell by his face that he'd totally forgotten how bad it tastes. Ha. He says, "So I bet you want to know how I know so much about it."

You have access to a computer? "Whatever."

"It's here. My dad has it. I heard him talking about it on the phone, to the CIA, maybe." He crosses his arms. "Or maybe the FBI."

Wait. The bell's in the house?

I'm in the house with the bell right now. My heart feels like I'm making it into a coffee smoothie.

I say, "What? Why does he have it?"

"Because he and the government are best buddies? I dunno. You know my dad. If I'm not cheery enough when I say good morning, he mumbles the rest of the day about sending me to military school. I don't ask questions."

"That's crazy that it's here."

"You can't tell *anyone*." His eyes go huge. "Listen. It's like . . . a huge secret."

I'm practically in the same house as Graham right now. I say, "Where is it?"

"I can't *tell* you! God, Wil, this is like a family secret. I never should have told you."

"But you wanted to show off," I say, but I can't make fun of him right now. My head isn't in it. Because right now I'm in the same house with tossing a baseball and staying up late watching scary movies and being tucked under his arm during nightmares and hurting my elbow when we wrestle and ice-cream sandwiches.

I close my eyes for a minute, because it's not like I'm going to cry or something in the middle of Anthony's kitchen.

Graham.

I don't think there's a way to convince Anthony to tell me where the bell is. He acts like a dog on his leash as far as his dad is concerned. I don't really blame him.

I've been friends with Anthony since wombhood, and I don't think I've talked to his dad more than a handful of times. And every time I've seen him, he's been yelling at someone. Usually Anthony. I'm not exaggerating: every single time. Even when he's on TV, he's usually yelling. I'm not exactly on a first name basis with Mrs. Lohen, either, but at least I'm used to her. She just wants to disinfect everything and watch soap operas, and she walks around with this face like she's preparing for a heart attack or a bout of food poisoning. Mr. Lohen, on the other hand, is a wild animal.

So there's no way Anthony's going to hand me the bell, when both of us know his dad might eat him alive if he's caught.

I'm going to have to steal it. I've never stolen anything, which is annoying right now. Experience would be useful. But I do know that there's no better time to steal something than when a guy's parents are asleep and all the lights are out and you're supposed to be hunting around.

See where I'm going with this?

I say, "So my parents won't let me have sleepovers again until I'm like twenty-five. Can we all come over here tomorrow night?"

Anthony's eyes are about to fall out of his head. "Are you joking?" He looks into his living room, where all the knickknacks are arranged like trophies. The TV's covered with a blanket, because it's not TV-time so it has to take a nap, and there's plastic over the couch. I bet under the beds in Anthony's house, all the dust bunnies are folded like clean laundry.

I totally understand why having a sleepover here is a ridiculous idea, since our ideas of midnight activities aren't Lohen-approved, like crocheting or teeth flossing. But that's not relevant to my plan.

My brain's flopping around in my head trying to think of ways to bribe Anthony when his dad comes downstairs with his gray hair all messed up and his glasses perched on top of his head like they're goggles and he's about to go swimming. He makes his shocked face—it's a lot like Anthony's—at the mess in the kitchen.

"Do you have *any idea* how wasteful this is, Anthony?" he screams. "How much money you've eviscerated and sprayed around our kitchen?"

Anthony stays absolutely still. He doesn't even look down. When my dad's mad at me, the last thing I can do is make eye contact. It's like we're the wrong sides of a magnet and my eyes are repelling his.

But Anthony's staring right at his dad, pretending to be calm, but I can see that he's scared just because I know him so well. His fingers are shaking a little.

Mr. Lohen picks up the lid of the blender and throws it at the sink. Or toward Anthony, it's hard to tell, but Anthony doesn't flinch. Mr. Lohen screams, "Why don't you get down on the floor and lick up this mess, because you're not eating in this house until you've earned every cent you've thrown away with your little game here!"

Anthony doesn't get down on the floor.

Mr. Lohen goes on and on. It's like he doesn't know Eben and I are here. All he can see is Anthony and how angry Anthony makes him.

Eben and I make awkward, but really necessary, eye contact. He shrugs a little. What can we do? I feel like we should leave, but I'm worried if I even twitch, Mr. Lohen will go after me like a lion after a gazelle. It's best to sit here and pretend I'm dead or invisible. Eben seems to agree.

It doesn't seem like Mr. Lohen's ever going to stop,

but then Luke comes downstairs and grabs him by the shoulder, hard enough that Mr. Lohen loses his balance and stumbles backward a little.

"Enough," Luke says.

Whoa.

They stare at each other like they're about to fight. This is the first time I've noticed how tall Luke is. Graham was little; I'm almost as tall as he was when he died, and Anthony isn't big either. But Luke has four inches on Mr. Lohen, easy.

And I think they both know it.

Mr. Lohen turns to Anthony and goes, "You better have cleaned up every last speck of food in here by the time your mother tries to cook dinner!" Then he storms downstairs to his secret laboratory or whatever.

"You okay?" Luke says.

I look at Anthony. He hasn't moved much. To be honest, I totally wouldn't blame him if he cried right now. Eben and I would probably be nice enough to pretend he didn't. And I know Luke would let it go.

But Anthony takes a minute and looks around the kitchen. The expression on his face is like he doesn't see the mess, or at least that it totally doesn't concern him. Then he says, "So. Zombie Tag here tomorrow?"

I grin. "Absolutely. You going to play with us, Luke?" I guess I'm saying thank you for saving Anthony.

Luke looks up at me, his eyebrows together. "You think I'm going to stay in and play tag? On a Saturday night?" He chuckles while he wipes down the countertops.

I can't sleep.

I don't have nightmares anymore, but I used to all the time. Even before Graham died. They were always about stupid stuff he used to scare me with when I was awake. Or about getting lost. A lot of the time, about getting lost.

I used to sleepwalk, too, and sometimes I'd blame the sleepwalking when I ended up in Graham's room after a nightmare, even though most of the times I walked there I was fully awake and shaking and begging him to do something.

Graham had nightmares sometimes, too. He said when we were really little, we had this babysitter who accidentally left us in a car for a long time. After that, he didn't like being shut in. He never locked a door.

I don't remember getting stuck in the car. But I do

know that the haunted house on the corner at Halloween only made me scream the year Graham was at a party instead of with me, and that somehow I always ended up squished in the armchair next to him during car chase scenes in movies, even though he'd try to push me off and tell me I was too clingy. I guess I liked having him around when I was scared.

I'd go into his room and say, "Graham?"

He'd crack his eyes open. "God, Wil, what?"

"Please?"

He'd think about it for a minute, watching me. "I have a test tomorrow."

"I'll be so quiet."

"You're getting kind of old for this."

I'd give him my smallest smile. "I'm a kid forever, remember?"

He'd chuckle and sigh and push back the covers so I could get in. I would crawl into bed next to him and snuffle against the mattress until he gave me a corner of his pillow.

"Tell me a story?" I'd ask.

And he would nod and roll onto his back, his eyes still closed. "Once upon a time there was a magical world where nobody ever got lost."

"Nobody *ever*."

"Ever."

I would lie awake and let that sit in my head, while Graham, too tired to finish the story, stroked my hair until he fell asleep, his palm pressed against my forehead.

And getting lost, being alone, that was what scared me, but him . . . See, he really, really hated being shut in, and now I don't have nightmares, because I can't sleep, because I'm lying awake thinking about him sealed up in a box and buried under the ground.

BEFORE I GO OVER to Anthony's house for the night, I have to make sure I'm prepared for whatever happens. This isn't just an ordinary game of Zombie Tag. I pack my ski mask and my bug spray, which Graham and I ruled out as a zombie weapon because it bothered his asthma, but might be necessary for a zombie night this extreme. Besides, even though Graham and I practiced fighting zombies together, I made up Tag on my own. I'm allowed to change the rules without asking him.

Because tonight I'm ringing the bell, and everyone buried within five miles will wake up. It will be the moment I've been waiting for. The zombie infestation.

And after that, no one really knows what's going to happen.

That's no problem. I'm prepared for anything.

While I'm putting my supplies into my backpack, I see myself in the mirror. I reach out and put my hand over where my face is.

I look scary. I look like a trained zombie killer. Which is good. That's what I'm supposed to be. And it's really cool.

Until one of those zombies is your brother.

Do I really have it in me to take down Graham? My heart starts to speed up, so I close my eyes and imagine myself somewhere else until I calm down. I'm with Anthony. We're skateboarding. It's really sunny. It's okay.

But then I let my mind drift over to Graham, and I'm sizing him up like a cow in a butcher shop, trying to figure out if I could beat him.

He was really strong. My parents wouldn't let us wrestle because I always ended up getting my head smashed into the floor, even when Graham was trying to be gentle.

But he doesn't stand a chance against my well-practiced zombie fighting skills. Even if he comes back with the knowledge of all the techniques he taught me, he's still going to be unarmed and unprepared. Not like me.

Fighting the other zombies will be easy. But if this

were a movie, Graham would be my downfall. I'd get all sentimental right when he's about to eat me, and my brain would start playing this montage of us playing hockey together or talking about girls, with meandering violin music in the background, so I'd decide to give him a chance, to see if I could tame him, and then—WHAM!—I'd be eaten alive by my own brother.

I can't let that happen. I'm hoping, obviously, that Graham springs out of that coffin as good as new, and that zombies aren't the things we decided they were. They're just people. Alive again. It would make a really lame movie, yeah. But a really good real life.

But what if they aren't?

Then I've killed everyone.

I'm thinking too fast again.

He's going to come back and he's going to be fine and normal, so I'm allowed to stop thinking about killing him. I don't need to think about this.

Then my phone rings. It's Stella. "Can you bring my backpack to Anthony's?" she asks me.

Stella has a secret backpack loaded with all her sleepover supplies. Her book of scary stories, her flashlight, the twenty dollar spatula her mom thinks her aunt borrowed. She can't keep the backpack at her house, so we drag it around from place to place with her. Stella lives this whole double life. She isn't allowed to stay over at boys' houses, so she always has to tell her mom she's sleeping over at Mary Cavender's, where she definitely wouldn't need zombie weapons.

I only know all of this because I guess I like hearing about Mary Cavender. It's not a big deal or anything.

So I say, "Are you going over to Mary's for real soon?"

"You're so creepy."

"I'm just being a good friend. We're having a dialogue right now. This is a true sign of our friendship."

"Mary and I aren't even friends anymore."

"But she's . . ." I don't know. She has really nice hair.

"She just wants to read magazines and paint her toenails. Do you still have that water gun? Let's drench Eben when he falls asleep."

I have to give her credit; she knows how to get my mind somewhere else. And after we hang up, and I try to go back to thinking about Graham; it's hard for some reason. My brain wants to stick on Stella. I have to work to get back to what I really should be concentrating on.

Graham. Once he's back, I'll have to go find him. I'll have to think of some excuse to tell the Lohens so they'll let me leave in the middle of the night. I guess I'll fake a

stomachache. I probably can't use that dead iguana excuse twice.

My father comes to my door and says, "Who was
that on the phone?"

"Stella."

"She's a nice girl."

"I guess."

I think that's when he notices I'm packing. He frowns
hard, even though I hid all the zombie stuff at the bottom of my bag.

I say, "I guess I didn't ask if I could go over to Anthony's."

"You assumed you weren't grounded?"

"Am I?"

"No." He cracks a bit of a smile. It's one of those
warm ones that makes him look older than he is. I like
those. I smile, too, as I go back to my packing.

He comes into my room and sits on the bed. Ever
since I started hiding those magazines in various spots in
my room, I've been anxious whenever one of my parents
comes inside. My eyes are darting to all the places the
magazines are hidden. I feel like an idiot sometimes for
having printed evidence. My friends look at stuff on
their phones like it's their job. Don't get me wrong, I've

looked, and there's some all right stuff online, but I prefer the magazines. I guess I'm a retro sort of man. Call me classy.

And to be honest, I don't think I care if Mom and Dad know all my secrets, as long as they promise to die without ever letting on that they know.

Dad says, "I guess you wouldn't consider spending a night at home with your mom and me?"

"I'm home all the time."

"We were talking about making a ton of popcorn and trying to get through as many stupid comedies as we could in one night."

"You'll have fun."

He looks at me for a second, then says, "Wil, can we talk?"

"It's nothing personal. I just already have these plans. You need to learn to take rejection better, Dad."

"Wil. Listen. I just want you to know that if you have questions about what's going on in the world, you can ask me."

I don't mean to be a jerk, but that is such bull. If I ask any questions at all, my dad tells me I'm never going to be able to get a job if the government finds out I type "zombies" into search engines over and over again, and my mom suggests we all do family counseling.

Plus, none of my questions are anything he would be able to answer.

He says, "Your mom and I aren't living under the delusion that this has been an easy six months for you. We're trying to support you any way we can."

Also, I hate when my parents reveal their motives to me. Don't tell me you're trying to support me. Just do it. Then I can't feel guilty when it doesn't work.

He's expecting me to talk so I say, "Thanks, Dad."

We used to talk about things. Real things. I'm not saying we sat down every day and had man-to-man talks about life and the universe and the meaning of whatever, but if I had a problem at school, we'd talk about it. Or if I had a fight with Graham and I was mad about it, he'd listen to my side and tell me smart things that reminded me that Dad is pretty old and that's okay. Because old means maybe a lot less soul but definitely a little more brain, and that's good to have around sometimes. Even if you never, ever want it to happen to you.

Now he says, "I know I've been busy with work, but after this quarter, things will be slowing down."

I don't know what 'quarter' actually means, but it must be slang for *years and years and years*, because he's always saying that.

I'm about to suggest that when I get home tomorrow,

he and I go outside and work on my pitching, but then I remember tomorrow, for better or for worse, Graham will come back. Tomorrow is going to be really different.

I know it would be incredibly stupid, but right now I want to tell him so badly that I feel it pulling in my stomach. I want him to tell me if I'm doing the right thing.

But then I take one more look at his screwed-up, broken smile and I know that I am. Because the chance that I'm serving us all up as a zombie feast is worth it for this chance that Graham will be back and we will be normal again. Because the grief counselor was wrong, it turns out. We can't live without him.

So when he says, "I love you," I just nod in response, because I'm thinking about how the next time he says that, he'll really mean it. Because he'll be my real dad again.

ANTHONY GETS MAJOR POINTS for having the game here in the first place, so I don't judge too hard when he shushes me the second I walk in, even though I happen to know his father sleeps with these really massive earplugs. Anthony and I used to steal them and use them as spare soldiers in our toy armies.

Everyone's gathered in the living room, drinking soda and grinning like criminals. I toss Stella's backpack on the ground, and she nods at me as she finishes folding up the Post-it Notes. I open mine. POOR DEFENSE-LESS HUMAN (BARRICADE) it says inside.

This is the first time ever that I'm happy I'm not the Zombie. It would be hard to effectively search the house if I was distracted by my craving for brains. We move into a circle and close our eyes. When the Zombie taps me on my back, I count to ten and open my eyes. I grab my spatula. "I'm going solo."

"You're going to be zombie food, man," Stella says.

I say, "I'm the master. Zombies are going down." I click off my flashlight before I walk out of the living room, so they can tell I have zero desire to be followed. I'm a lone ranger tonight.

I have this secret fantasy that I'll find the bell so quickly that I'll still find the Key and escape before everyone. That's two zombie victories in one.

I think about where the bell might be. Anthony's house has the exact same layout as my old one, so I know Mr. Lohen doesn't have an office. My dad said we moved so that he could have working space, but really we all knew we were moving to get away from where Graham died. But none of us said it.

Sometimes I wonder if Eben ever thinks about my brother when he's brushing his teeth in that bathroom.

I'm going to have to cross my fingers that Mr. Lohen hasn't hidden the bell in his bedroom, because there's no way I can get in there. I need some good luck. That's all I need. I'll bring the raw skill. The universe just needs to root for me a little bit on this one. For me and Graham. I need some good karma for the sake of brothers everywhere right now, because brothers should be to-gether, and I'm trusting the universe to know that.

When my dad has something I'm not supposed to see, like a birthday present or a power tool, he hides it in the basement. I run down and swing my flashlight from corner to corner. Anthony's house is immaculate even down here. There aren't any piles of junk to sift through. There's no place to hide anything. No way the Key is down here.

Someone screams upstairs, and I probably lose a year of my life from the full two seconds my heart stops beat-ing. But Mr. Lohen must be wearing some really good earplugs, because I don't hear any angry footsteps, just undead ones.

I head toward the bathroom—maybe the medicine cabinet?—and trip over a loose floorboard. I hit the floor hard.

Upstairs, Anthony calls, "Braaaaaaaaaaains."

Uh oh. They got Anthony. I need to hurry.

I'm clambering to my feet when I realize that this isn't the kind of basement that would just happen to have a loose floorboard. Everything here is perfect, ex-cept one board? It doesn't make sense.

I grab my flashlight and shine it at the floorboard.

The edge I tripped over doesn't line up how it should. My fingers are small, so I can fit them into the crack and pry up the board.

At first I don't see anything, then my flashlight beam hits a shoebox tucked underneath the boards.

Jackpot.

"Braaaaaaaains!" The zombies are almost at the top of the stairs.

My fingers are shaking, so it takes me a minute to dig through the cotton balls before I find the bell. I unwrap it from layers and layers of plastic wrap. Someone went through a lot of trouble to make sure this bell stayed silent.

It's so much smaller than I'd expected. It's blue and gold and fits in my palm. The gold rim is decorated and delicate, like it's braided from thread. My fingers hit an inscription on the side, and I raise my flashlight so I can read it. *Ring 10 times for a shift.*

A shift.

There's a little blue notebook in the box with the bell. I guess it's an instruction manual or something. But I know how this thing works. I did the research. And the zombies are coming down the stairs, and I don't have time to admire this bell or read a little book about it or think too much, so I stuff the notebook in my pocket and okay, here goes, I close my eyes and ring the bell.

I think I did something wrong. I was expecting something loud, or at least distinctive. This sounded just like when my mom shakes her keys at us so we'll hurry up. But I keep going anyway. Ten times. God, what if it doesn't work? Do I need to be outside? Maybe I got this all wrong . . .

Before I can work it out, I hear footsteps crashing down the stairs. Time's up.

I replace the empty box and the floorboard, stick the bell in my pocket, and switch off my flashlight. I don't see a couch or a cabinet or anything big to hide behind, so I just flop down on the ground behind a column and play dead.

"Braaaaaains," they're all chanting as they come down to the basement. God, it's all of them. There goes my chance of escaping notice.

I'm the last human, and I have no idea where the Key is. Now I can't remember what we're even using for the Key. I have no idea how to get out of this house.

"Soooooo hungry," Eben moans. "Neeeeeeed braaaaaains."

There's no way Eben's biting me. No way.

I don't think they've seen me, but they're getting closer and closer. I'm going to have to sprint through them and hope I somehow run straight into the Key and out of the house and to my brother. It sounds totally impossible, but it's my only shot.

I jump to my feet and they all groan in surprise. I sprint toward the stairs, switching my flashlight on and off quickly to confuse them. Zombies can't stand flashing lights.

But they're moving faster than they should, and I feel them on the back of my neck. At the top of the stairs, I spin around to try to fend them off with my spatula, but I trip, again. This time it's not a loose floorboard; it's the top of the stairs.

I land hard, and I hear the bell shatter. It's louder when it breaks than when it rings, but the guys and Stella probably can't hear it over their thirst for flesh.

I don't have time to worry about the bell, because they're closing in on me. And it's scarier than it's ever been. It's too close to real. Any minute, the real zombies could be on top of me, too.

I scream and swing my spatula at them, but it's no use. They're about to get me; their mouths are getting closer and closer. I'm zombie food, zombie food—

The front door opens.

Anthony straightens up. "What the—"

It's probably just Luke coming home from his date.

The others stop and look toward the door. "Anthony, what's up, man? We're about to get Wil."

Anthony keeps staring at the door, his eyes enormous.

As soon as I've caught my breath, I sit up enough to follow Anthony's eyes. And sure enough, it's Luke. But he's pale, and that woman next to him doesn't look like his date. She's dirty and hunched over, her hair curled on top of her head.

Anthony whispers, "*Grandma?*"

Oh my God. It worked.

"Get back!" I yell to my friends. They scurry around me and we stand together and brandish our spatulas. I've trained them well.

I hear Stella breathing next to me. "Don't you dare try anything," she calls out.

Anthony's grandmother blinks at us.

It's a trap.

We're ready.

I'm ready. My hand might be shaking on my spatula, but I'm ready.

Luke says, "I just found her . . ."

She yawns and sits down at the table. "Don't suppose you have some tea, Lucas?"

The silence rings out, and nobody moves. Anthony's grandmother doesn't bare her teeth or lunge out of her kitchen chair.

Stella's arm relaxes a little. I feel my heart slowing down. And I'm warming with the realization that I actually did this. Anthony's grandmother's been dead since we were in first grade.

They're actually back.

Which means Graham is somewhere right now.

Mrs. Lohen comes down the stairs, rubbing her face. I think her eye makeup might be tattooed on, which is even scarier than the zombie in the kitchen.

She stops at the kitchen door and stares. We're too frozen to even flinch when she screams her husband's name and runs up the stairs to get him.

"Uh-oh," David says. Eben looks like he's about to pee himself, and even Stella's starting to sweat.

Zombies aren't nearly as scary as the possibility of Mr. Lohen eating us alive.

Anthony's grandmother studies us like she's bored, then says, "Lucas, how about that tea?"

MR. LOHEN DOESN'T come down screaming and spitting like we expect. He gets to the bottom of the stairs and goes straight into the kitchen without looking at us. His arm is around his wife and he's smiling like he has extra teeth. "Martha!" he exclaims. "How lovely! How incredibly miraculous to have you back!" I guess being a smooth-talking politician comes in handy in these types of situations.

While everyone else is distracted, we turn and face each other. Anthony is glaring at me, hard. He's hiding something behind his back, but I can't see what. Probably a punch in the face with my name on it.

I mouth, "Sorry." That doesn't seem to make him any happier. I didn't really think it would.

I'll worry about that later.

David says, "Oh my God, what is going on?" He looks at me like he wants me to explain things. He would trust me with anything, I think, which makes him cool but kind of stupid.

Stella whispers, "This is crazy. I went to her funeral."

"This is a dream," Eben says. His voice is quivering. God, if I'm going to keep calling Anthony a drip, I need to find a whole new word for Eben.

"She's not acting like a zombie," David says. "She sounded normal when she talked."

Stella looks at him. "We don't know what a real zombie is, idiot. Did you really think they'd be like we just were in the game?"

I wish she hadn't said that. It's not that we didn't know that it was a game. It's just that this feels kind of like they're calling me a liar.

And none of this is what I need to be thinking about right now.

Graham. Graham. Graham.

I need to get out of here now, but the front door is so far away and I can't get to it without passing through the kitchen. And I'm still afraid that any second I'm going to hear Anthony's grandmother start growling and writhing, but so far it's just Mrs. Lohen fussing over her mother and asking her if she's warm enough and if she needs anything. And I hear Grandma Zombie calmly asking for tea over and over.

Then Luke comes out and says, "Dad wants to talk to you all in the basement."

Here it comes.

Luke leads us all down to the basement. He squeezes my shoulder, and Anthony's, but when Anthony tries to cling to him, Luke shrugs him away.

"I'm scared," Eben says. Wow, shocking.

But a minute later, Mr. Lohen storms downstairs. His smile has vanished. And for a second, the sentence *I've got to go find Graham* gets replaced with *Okay, I'm scared, too.* Because his fists are clenched and his jaw is locked shut, and he looks like he's about to line us up and shoot us until someone confesses.

"*Which one of you rang that bell?*" he yells.

I'm ready for Anthony to sell me out, but he doesn't. Everyone's glancing back and forth between Mr. Lohen and the stairs. I don't know if they're planning an escape or still preparing for Anthony's grandmother to run down and eat our brains.

I think I'm the first one to realize that this isn't a game.

"*Which one of you?*" Mr. Lohen says.

Luke says, "Dad, look. I'm sure it was an accident." He's rubbing his forehead, and he looks really tired.

Mr. Lohen swings his glare around to each of us. "Who was down in the basement?"

"We all were, Dad," Anthony says. Except they were all down here only for a second, and they're figuring that out now. I hope Eben's too dumb to work this out. He's the only one who I'm scared wouldn't cover for me.

He worked it out. He glances at me, and I send him the best death stare I have. *If you tattle, I'll tell everyone about that time you tried to make a peephole into the girls' locker room.*

Luke says, "Look, it's done. Can't you just fix it?"

Mr. Lohen turns to him and goes, "*No, I can't fix it! I cannot just fix it.*"

I do everything I can to stop shaking. It's done. There's no point in second thoughts now. It's done. They're back.

Mr. Lohen and Luke are staring at each other just like they did yesterday in the kitchen. Mr. Lohen looks like he's remembering, again, that Luke is bigger than he is. Anthony says that ever since Luke's growth spurt, his dad's stayed off his case. I hope Anthony grows soon.

Everything's quiet for a minute, and I can hear one of Anthony's neighbors screaming. I wonder who just came home.

Graham is probably waking up my parents right now. I hope they don't freak out and hurt him.

Luke says. "Okay, then . . . that sucks."

Mr. Lohen leans heavily against the beam. "Yes. Yes, Lucas. *That sucks.*"

Luke laughs a little. "You're so fired."

"Thank you, Lucas. Thank you very much for your *helpful remarks*!"

"Can I go home?" I say softly.

Mr. Lohen looks at me. "What? Need to bring the bell back to your father? Trying to infiltrate my department, is that it? Did he send you here?"

Whoa.

Luke says, "Dad, come on. Wil wouldn't steal it."

I say, "It's just that I think maybe my brother will be there. And since it doesn't look like they're coming back with guns or anything . . ."

Luke takes his attention off his father and stares at me. "Oh my God. Graham's home."

"I don't see why he wouldn't be," I say. I bet I'm making the same face right now that he is. I have this urge to run to him and hug him, but I don't do it. I think Mr. Lohen would kill me.

David says, in this small voice, "Does that mean my dad's back?"

I'd completely forgotten that David's dad was dead. Now I feel horrible.

Mr. Lohen growls, "Only if he was buried in the cemetery on Blackwell. The bell has a five-mile radius."

David says, "Oh," and looks down.

I should have rung the bell somewhere different, where it would have woken up David's dad *and* Graham. Now it's too late. I feel the broken pieces shift in my pocket.

Mr. Lohen narrows his eyes at David. "Disappointed, are you?"

Luke says, "Of course he's disappointed, Dad, God. He thought his dad . . ."

Mr. Lohen stands up and roars, "*Stole my bell so you could see your father, did you?*"

David stutters, "I-I didn't—"

I feel a hand on my shoulder. It's Luke. He says, "Dad, shut up and go see Grandma. It's done."

Mr. Lohen looks like he's about to hit Luke, but Luke pulls back his shoulders and Mr. Lohen actually shrinks away from him.

That's weird.

What's even weirder is how his face changes while he looks at Luke, then when he looks at us. He's gone from angry to terrified in less than thirty seconds.

And he mutters something like, "I've got to go," and runs upstairs. He has a weird run, like a kid.

Luke says, "I learned a long time ago that I could do that." He smiles down at me. "Ever since I got bigger than him, he backs down every time we argue. Doesn't usually get that freaked out, though."

Anthony offers this weak little laugh, but when I look at him, he has his glare back on. I know I should apologize again, but I'm not sorry right now. I'm not anything but dying to see my brother.

"Who needs a ride home?" Luke asks.

"Not me," Stella says. "Mom would herniate if a teenager drove me anywhere."

Eben whispers, "Are we supposed to stay in this house with a *zombie*?" But everyone ignores him.

Luke smiles at me again. "I bet *you* do."

I breathe. "I do. I really, really, really, really do."

I glance at Anthony's grandmother on my way out. She's just sipping tea and yawning while Mrs. Lohen tells her about how both boys made honor roll. I know I should be scared, but I'm not. I don't know how to

63

explain it, but it somehow feels normal that she's here. It feels right.

Luke lets me pick the music in his car. I'm expecting him to drive quickly, since his dead best friend is just a few miles away. But he drives like he's trying to pass a test to get his license. All his movements are so precise. He clicks on the turn signal with a careful flick of his hand. I want to scream at him to hurry up.

He says, "You took a big risk stealing that bell, you know?"

I think about denying it, but what's the point? I know Luke is on my side. "I know," I say.

"Besides the danger of my father ripping out your organs one by one . . . God, what makes you think Graham will even be normal?"

"I don't." But I didn't know how things could be worse than they were.

I'm smiling without trying to.

"Pretty brave," Luke says, but like he isn't really sure that's a good thing.

I say, "But it worked out. Your grandmother seemed okay. She wasn't dripping blood or anything."

If I screwed up, if I made a huge mistake, for some reason I'm sure Luke will tell me right now.

But he says, "Looks like you did okay, kid. Except now we have to deal with my grandmother again."

I laugh a little, but now that I've really let myself think about Graham, there's no going back.

I actually pulled this off. And aside from Mr. Lohen being royally angry at me, nothing bad happened. I guess the broken bell could end up being a problem, but only if I wanted to be some kind of crusader going around the world waking up dead people. And that sounds like a time-suck anyway.

I'm about to get home and my brother's going to be there. And I know it, and I feel it, and I want to roll my head back and scream as loudly as I can and throw my arms up in the air and stand on something really tall. Because everything is going to be all right now. It's not like Graham was perfect all the time, and it's not like we always got along. Most of the time he didn't want me around. But we were best friends when we were kids, and I always knew we were going to be best friends again someday.

And now we're going to be. How could he ever blow me off again? I just saved his life. This is almost as good as rescuing him during the asthma attack. This is the next best thing.

Luke pulls up at my house and parks. "Go see your brother," he says.

"Aren't you coming?"

Luke looks up at the house. He opens and closes his hands a few times, like he's getting ready to go up to bat.

Then he says, "No, I don't think I should. I'll give you and your parents some time. I'll come over tomorrow."

This is very nice and all, to let us see him first, but I don't get it. If it were Anthony—even Anthony in his current murderous state—instead of Graham, I'd be shoving Luke out of the way to get through the door. I can't understand being reasonable at a time like this. This is a time for screaming and hugging.

Luke can be this rational because he's so old. He's almost seventeen, whoa.

I scramble out of the car and up my front steps. It takes me four tries to get my key to fit in the lock, my hands are so excited.

I open the door as Luke's car pulls away. "Graham?"

And there he is, sitting at the kitchen table with my parents. They have their hands all over him, touching the shirt I made sure he was wearing when they buried him, the yellow one with the stripe that makes him look

66

like Charlie Brown and made all the adults mumble about how he should have been in a suit.

Graham.

I forgot about the freckles on his forehead.

I forgot about the eye that's a darker brown than the other one.

I forgot about his fingernails and his ugly knuckles and his shoulders too big for his shirts and all the imperfect details you don't notice when he's just the guy in the next bedroom or the grin in the pictures you look at again and again and again.

Mom says, "Wil, oh my God, honey, look. Can you believe . . ."

Graham looks up at me. "Hello."

He doesn't smile. I want to wait for the smile, but I'm running across the kitchen with my legs pumping as hard as they will go. I throw myself at Graham, and I'm a torpedo and he's my brother and I'm holding him so tight and later we'll pretend this didn't happen and we're strong and big and we don't cry, but right now I don't ever want to stop hugging him, ever.

He doesn't hug me back. He stays totally still, and when I look up, he's watching me, his mouth pinched and his eyebrows drawn together.

"What are you doing?" he says, like he's only slightly interested.

I wish he wouldn't act too cool for me right now. This really isn't the time. Now I want to hit him while I'm hugging him. "Stop it."

He touches my cheek like he isn't sure it's there.

I say, "Graham, are you kidding? It's me. It's *Wil*."

"I know who you are." He sips his tea, then looks at Mom and Dad. "Why is he crying?"

I can't believe he's making fun of me for this right now. He deserves for me to drag him to the floor and punch him and beat him up and embarrass him right back, except I know he would tackle me and have me pinned in a second, just like always. Just like always, just the same. Nothing different.

My hand is on his arm. He's so real. I say, "Shut up, man. This isn't the . . . don't play around right now."

"I'm not playing." His eyes don't look away from mine. They're all brown and no smile.

My stomach starts to hurt. "Graham, don't give me that, okay? I'm so happy you're . . ."

He tilts his head to the side.

Maybe he doesn't remember. That could make sense. I say, "You were dead. You were totally dead. And now you're back."

"I know that," he says.

I say. "So don't you feel—"

Dad says, "Wil, right now Graham isn't feeling—"

"I don't feel anything," Graham says. He shrugs and drinks his tea.

But he's here. He's right in front of me. I see him. His arm is in my hand. I can feel him.

I squeeze his arm, hard, and he says, "That hurts," like he doesn't care.

"It hurts."

I was crying and holding my skinned knee, crying because I was still such a baby when I was seven.

"Yeah, looks like." Graham crouched down next to me, studying my scrape like there was going to be a test on it.

"It hurts. It hurts soooo much."

"Okay." He took my hand and squeezed it. "Man up for me. I'm going to do some magic."

"Promise?"

"Yeah, I promise. Hold on." He thought for a moment, then said, "Okay. Close your eyes hard."

I squeezed them as much as I possibly could, and I

69

gripped his hand, but my knee didn't feel any better. I opened my eyes and said, "Fix it!"

He still had his face scrunched in concentration. "I'm working on it."

My knee twinged again. "*Fix it!*"

He opened his eyes and his chin shook. He looked young and afraid and out of options. Over a stupid skinned knee.

HE KEEPS WATCHING ME like a statue. I can't do this.

I thought I'd be glued to Graham's side for ages, telling him everything he's missed and showing him my new room and listening to him breathe. But the second he turns away from me and starts listening, blankly, to Mom babbling about how she'll have to wash some sheets for him, I'm gone. I think maybe I'm going to throw up, but I end up in my room instead.

I can hear him through the walls, answering their questions in the world's shortest sentences. I should be smiling just from hearing his voice.

But he used to chatter all through dinner. I'd have a story about school I'd saved up all day, and I couldn't ever tell it because he never shut up. It used to make me so mad. He was full of so many words all the time.

I want him here with stories about what underground was like. I want him curious about me. I want Graham. I did this for *Graham*.

It's like someone ate his brain. Or his heart.

So now I'm hiding under my covers and I don't want to get up for anything, because I don't want to cry again. Not over Zombie-Graham.

I feel someone sit on my bed, and I slowly take the covers off my head. Dad.

"It's three a.m.," I tell him. "I'm supposed to be asleep."

He laughs a little. "Is that how this conversation goes? Seems a little off to me."

"So you should probably leave me alone and let me sleep or rot or something."

He doesn't say anything for a few minutes, but he brings his hand up to my head and strokes my hair, kind of roughly, like he's trying to push it back into my head. He doesn't look at me. He's tired.

Eventually he says, "Any idea how this happened?"

I shake my head, maybe too hard. But I'm scared he knows it was me. It's a pretty huge coincidence that we were just talking about zombies and here they are.

He gives me a small smile. He doesn't think I could do this. I'm his kid.

Except then he says, "Well, there's no law against ringing that bell. Whoever did it might be hounded by the press, if he turns himself in, but I doubt he'll get in any real trouble."

Oh. "He probably shouldn't turn himself in, still."

"No." He's still stroking my hair. "Probably not."

Okay, I should stop calling my dad lame. Maybe I need to reevaluate the way I think about people. Dad can be kind of cool. Anthony can be brave. Graham can be calm. No.

Dad says, "Well. This is pretty incredible, huh? Seeing him again. I forgot he was so little." That's not really fair. Graham's short, but his shoulders are big and he's strong. He's the best at football. The best.

Dad shifts on the bed, looking at something far away "Of course I'd hoped, wanted to believe there was some kind of possibility. But I never thought it would really happen. It didn't make sense to really think about it. If I ever started, I'd just . . ." He shakes his head a little.

I want to whisper, "I know." But I don't know, because I never gave up like he did. Instead I say, "He's not Graham."

"What?"

"It's not Graham." I cross my arms and roll so I'm

73

facing the wall and not him. "He didn't hug me back. He wasn't happy to see us." The real Graham is flashing through my head like a slideshow. Laughing shouting fishing cursing sobbing running drawing punching. My stomach hurts so much. I've never missed him like this. Not even at the funeral or on my birthday. Dad grips my shoulder, like he knows.

I say, "He didn't even care that I was crying." It feels like I have to push the words out of my lungs.

"He asked why."

"Yeah, like he was asking why I was home late from school."

Dad says, "We're blessed to have him back at all, you know that. We can't complain if he's not quite the same. This is a very unstudied . . ."

"Yes, I can complain! I can complain all I want!"

"Okay," he says quietly. "You can."

I sniff.

He's drumming out some kind of rhythm on my back. I think it's the lullaby he used to sing when I was a kid.

"What if he's dangerous?" I whisper.

Dad hugs me. "We know. We're prepared. Your mom and I put together emergency kits years ago. You're safe, I promise."

I don't have the heart to tell him that I know more about zombie fighting than he and Mom ever could. Besides, an attempted takeover isn't even the worst possibility. I say, "What if he's never normal again?"

Dad thinks about this for a long time. "I think there's a good possibility he will be. He's a little shell-shocked right now, you know? He's been through a lot, Wil. We can't expect him to be back as good as new his first night."

Okay. That makes sense. He's just scared. Like how he'd always be quiet the morning after a nightmare, and I'd have to pull him back to the real world again, because Graham was not supposed to be quiet.

Dad paws my head. "He's been through a very scary transition. Probably two very scary transitions if we count waking up. Maybe he will be normal eventually. He's not so very far away, is he? No extra heads." Dad smiles at me.

"You really think he'll go back to how he was?"

"Well . . . Well, there's no way to really know, is there? Just like we don't know what it's like to be dead, we don't know what it's like to come back. Graham and . . . and all of them. There are so few records of last time."

"Yeah, Dad, I know that."

Now I wish Graham were here for a different reason. I want him to help me deal with Zombie-Graham. He wouldn't be logical like Dad and Luke and all the rest of the old people. He'd be worried and thrilled and horrified and here with me. Real Graham felt everything so strongly and so loudly that he made me look like a stone sometimes.

Dad says, "And some of it is probably age, remember? Growing up, becoming more rational . . ."

I frown.

He says, "You and Graham had been a little detached for a while before he died, eh? He was focused on different things."

"He was just stupid about girls and stuff."

"He's four years older than you," Dad says.

"I *know* that."

"Even without the death separating you, that's a big difference. You don't think some of this is just age?"

"Graham's still a kid." He is. He promised me he always would be.

"You shouldn't expect him to be just like you because he's back." He's touching my head again. "He isn't twelve."

He's not listening. "I just want him to be Graham."

"Give him time." Dad kisses my forehead. "Let him work through everything he's been through, keep an open heart and an open mind, and we'll see how much he's really changed. Learn what being a zombie really means. Not quite like your game, I don't suppose?"

"He hasn't tried to bite me yet, at least."

Dad smiles. "Get some sleep. You had the right idea with that one. I'm sure there will be a lot to deal with tomorrow."

"Are you going to sleep?" I ask him.

"We . . . we're going to stay up for a little while and watch Graham," he says.

At first I think he means they're just going to marvel at his hands and his face and the fact that he's here. Then I realize he means he wants to make sure Graham doesn't go psycho and steal our knives and try to kill all of us. That makes my stomach hurt more, so I push it away. He closes my door and I lie there, still.

I brought Graham back from the dead, so I must be able to bring him back from his post-death freak out. It'll just take some skill, that's all. And if there's anything I'm good at, it's zombies.

77

I was so busy making plans about how to fix Graham that I kind of forgot to sleep, so it feels like I've only had my eyes closed for a minute when I hear helicopters looming over our town and dozens of voices out in our driveway. It's not even seven in the morning. I haven't been up this early since school let out.

No way I'm changing out of my pajamas. I don't care who's here. I'm too tired.

I stumble out of my bedroom and into the living room. It's so loud. There are trucks with loud engines running in the cul-de-sac and it sounds like the helicopters are landing in our front yard.

Graham's standing at the window, drinking coffee. He started drinking coffee a few months before he died, and I always thought it was so stupid. Now I like it because it makes him feel real, less like the fantasy Graham I've been picturing since he died. He's here, and he brought the bits of himself that I didn't like. Now we just need to get the good parts back, too.

"Hey," I say.

He nods at me. "Hello."

"I'm Wil, remember?"

"Yeah, Wil. I know who you are. Hi."

I smile at him until he looks up.

He says, "How'd you sleep? I could hear you up late talking to Dad." He sounds like he's reading from a script, and Graham was always a really bad actor. He was always a tree or a sheep in the school plays because he read lines like a dead body. Like a zombie.

But I say, "I slept okay, except everything was so, so loud outside. Jack Bandit hid under the bed."

"Mmm."

"So how'd you sleep?"

He sips. "Mom made me stay up for a while, but I eventually got some sleep. I was exhausted."

"Are you happy to be home?"

"Happy?" he says kind of absently while he looks out the window.

I say. "Yeah. You know that thing where your chest feels good and the sides of your mouth go up?"

"I know what happy is, Wil."

I stand beside him at the window. There's a blue van parked in front of our house, and my parents are talking to a pretty lady in a red suit. She holds a microphone in front of their faces, and a guy in a T-shirt holds a big fuzzy mike over their heads.

"Are Mom and Dad going to be on TV?" I say.

"Yeah. They've been to all the families who've had someone come back."

I go back to my room to comb my hair, then I come back and make myself some toast. I'm trying not to watch Graham, but it's hard. I'm pretty excited about our progress. We're having a conversation. He's bored, but he's doing it. And that's the first step.

So I say, "Don't you want to know about everything that's been going on here since you, uh, died?"

Graham looks at me. "Hmm?" He's taken a shower, so all the dirt and grime is off of him, and he looks like he's been alive forever.

"I had the best baseball season ever," I say. "And Anton Barrow came in second in the truck derby last month. I got his autograph. Wanna see?"

"Hmmm."

That's not an answer. "Do you want some toast?"

"Okay. Thanks."

I put a few slices of bread in the toaster. Is hunger a feeling? I'm trying to convince myself that it's a really good sign that Graham wants some toast.

I head back to the window. I touch Graham's arm, just to see what happens. He looks at me. He doesn't smile, but he doesn't pull away, either. "Yeah?"

"So what can I call you?" I say.

"Graham."

"No, I mean, in my head I called you a zombie. Like, you and the other . . . zombies."

"Zombie's fine. I don't care," he says. I see his lips starting to form those words, and I want to snatch them out of his mouth and break them.

I don't know what to say now. We're staring out the window together, watching a reporter primp Mom and Dad, and I realize I'm listening to him breathe.

"Did you take your meds?" I say, really soft.

He nods. "Mom went to the drugstore this morning."

"Kay. Good." I don't know if he can die twice. I'd rather not find out. Not that I think Graham would automatically die if he had another asthma attack. I'm not stupid. I've seen him have attacks and not die a million times.

I get that the bad attack was a freak thing, an accident, nothing Graham had ever been prepared for. I know. I know it way deep inside me.

Somewhere.

I clear my throat. "So do you know the other zombies? The ones who came back with you?"

"What? Wil, of course not."

"Oh. I thought maybe you hung out with them or something."

He shakes his head. "It's not like that."

"I guess I thought maybe it was like heaven in movies and stuff."

"Fluffy clouds?"

"Yeah."

Outside, the reporter thanks Mom and Dad and heads back into the van. I think my parents are about to come back inside, but instead they turn to a different reporter and start talking to her. I hear my dad's voice, so much louder than it needs to be. "It's amazing having him back. He's just how he used to be. Exactly the same. Nothing to be afraid of. This is such a great thing. There's no reason for anyone to be worried."

"I hope you don't kill us," I say, quietly.

"What?"

"Because of . . . you know. What you are."

"Oh. I haven't been planning on it."

"So if you bite me, will I turn into a zombie?"

"Wil, what?"

"Can you try it?"

He bites my shoulder. I wait for my insides to start

decaying and my brain to start shriveling. Nothing happens. I guess I expected that.

"So what's dying like?" I ask.

"It's like . . . nothing, really." He takes a sip from his mug. I guess he realizes I'm waiting for him to say more, because he says, "There's nothing and nobody else around. You don't have anyone to count on but yourself. And you don't want anything, so it doesn't really matter what you do. Because no matter what happens, nothing changes."

My chest feels so cold that I have to steal his coffee and take a sip, or I'm afraid I'm going to stop breathing or something. I swallow. I hate coffee. "That sounds awful."

He watches me drink. "You get used to it."

A minute later, the news crews come inside to talk to Graham. They bring cops and guns in case Graham tries to rip them limb from limb, and I'm scared for the first time this morning. Graham already told me he wasn't going to hurt me.

Now I'm worried they're going to hurt him.

"That's my brother, okay?" I tell one of the cops.

His hand is on his gun and his eyes are on Graham. "He's a zombie."

"He's not just any zombie. Trust me, okay? Don't shoot him. Not even in the legs or something, to disable him. No shooting. I know he's acting weird, but he's really my brother."

Mom says, "No one's going to shoot anyone, Wil." But she isn't looking at me either. She's licking her thumb and scrubbing Graham's cheek with it, over and over. Graham doesn't squirm like he should.

"Okay," the reporter says. She looks terrified but happy about it, like Anthony at a scary movie. "Let's get the family over here on the couch, okay?"

Mom and Dad settle down on either side of Graham. Why don't I get to be next to him? That's totally not fair. I'm going to be sitting on the end next to my mom like a little kid.

"Uh uh." This guy in a suit stops me with his hand on my shoulder. "Not you."

"She said family."

"Not you. Just the parents and the . . ." He waves his hand at Graham.

"I'm part of this family."

"Not the part we need to see on camera right now, okay?"

Dad says, "Bud, you stand there and make sure they

don't mess up the lighting." He gives me this grin with half of his mouth.

I frown at him, hard, and he weakens a little. He says, "I'm sorry. It's just safer to keep you on the sidelines of this one, Wil."

Well, that's great. Now I get to stand here and watch while they interview my parents and Graham, and Dad throws his arm around Graham and tells the reporters what a good boy he is, how happy he is to be back in the real world. None of them catches my eye between takes. They're not mentioning me in their answers. Mom's going on and on about how happy she is that her son is back, like they've been all alone these past six months since Graham died. I wonder if anyone watching this will think that this is a pretty big house for just the two of them. Then everyone will figure out they're all liars.

I cross my arms and narrow my eyes at them. If Mom and Dad so much as glance at me, I'm going to fry them with my laser vision. But they don't.

Look, I know I'm just a kid and I'm all alive and everything, but that doesn't mean I don't exist. This sucks.

And now I want to tell everyone that this is all because of me, that I'm the one who woke the dead, that I'm the real hero of this news story. But I'm not stupid.

Just because my dad said I wouldn't get in trouble doesn't mean it's true. Besides, I don't really want all this attention, all these cameras and airbrushed reporters in red suits. That's not why I did this.

But some attention from my family would be nice. Since I did this for us.

"I WANTED MORE TORNADOES," Stella says as we walk out of the theater. "A movie called *Tornadoes of Doom* should have more than, like, two."

"But the second one was intense, man." I suck up the rest of my soda and throw the cup in the trash. My eyes are still freaking out from the light. I always have to blink like an idiot for ten minutes when I leave a movie.

"Anthony told me there was supposed to be another tornado, but they cut it. Which was supposedly because it was too long, but I heard there was an accidental naked part. Like, this girl's shirt just blew up and ta da, naked. So they had to cut it."

"No way."

"Would I lie to you?"

This is why Stella is so cool. I say, "I wonder if it's on the Internet."

"Duh. Of course it is. But you'll have to wade through all the zombie stories. I tried to Google how to make a cake in a mug today and it was like, *did you mean, 'are zombies going to eat my children?'*"

"I can't believe Anthony missed this."

She doesn't say anything. It's really, really noticeable when Stella doesn't say anything.

So I nudge. "Because he was really excited about this movie. I mean, he doesn't just go looking up facts about naked people for no reason."

She's still quiet.

"See, that was a joke. Because, you know, he does."

"Look, Anthony's very supremely mad at you."

I guess this shouldn't surprise me. I haven't talked to him since the bell-stealing incident three days ago, and it's not like I thought he was pleased with me when I left that night. But I've been so wrapped up in my no-hearted brother that I've been trying not to worry about it. That's what today was supposed to be. A distraction, a good day with Anthony and Stella. And then Anthony blew us off, and now he's ruining the day because I'm mad at him for being mad at me.

Though I guess I deserve it.

"So you stole the bell, I guess," Stella says. We're outside waiting for my mom and there's no one else around, but I still wish she wouldn't shout it out like that.

I say, "I mean . . . yeah."

"I guess he's not happy about that."

"Yeah."

"I don't know. I talked to him yesterday and he didn't even sound that mad. Just . . . weird and depressed and kind of scared. I guess the zombies are stressing him out. You should call him."

"Yeah." I nod. "Yeah."

Right now, though, I just want to go home. I'm anxious about spending this much time away. I'm trying to get Graham accustomed to me. I'm loud and excited when he's around so maybe I can rub off on him. And Mom and Dad keep letting people hound him whenever I'm not around. They even brought him to the doctor to do all these tests. They all came out normal, except that when they tried to prick his finger for blood, they couldn't break his skin. That's all over the news now.

I hope they start using a different zombie as their guinea pig. I heard Mom telling Dad that this had to stop, that she didn't want him to have any more tests, that they had to stop treating Graham like an animal. Which I thought was weird, because Graham's sort of a robot right now, which is the opposite of an animal.

While we're standing here waiting, I'm getting a few looks and whispers from kids at my school. They're taking wide paths away from me. I guess they saw Graham on the news.

"It's not like I'm a zombie," I say.

"Doesn't matter. Your family's contaminated." Stella sticks a piece of gum in her mouth. "Mom told me she doesn't want me talking to you anymore."

"So I guess she doesn't know you're here."

"She thinks I'm getting a manicure with Mary." She waves her gnawed fingernails in my face.

I wish Stella's mom and the people on the news were the only crazy ones, but it's been a week and the zombies are still everything anyone's talking about. My parents' friends called last night and uninvited them to their dinner party. This girl at school tried to go grocery shopping with her zombie dad and they got turned away at the register. One of our neighbors is putting up a high fence between their house and ours.

We're trying to ignore it, to hunker down and get on as close to normal as we can. We eat meals like a family and watch movies together on the couch, though Graham keeps leaving for his room or falling asleep in the middle of them. I keep reading books and trying to talk to him. My dad only leaves the house to go to work, and Mom stays home and does lesson plans and babysits Graham, who does nothing but eat and stare at the TV and give in when some reporter asks him do something. We decided not to let Graham out of the house on his own, which is never a problem, because he doesn't want to go anywhere. He still hasn't seen Luke, even though Luke called twice.

But the outside world is leaking in on us. Even if you avoid the news channels, which I try to do, there are commercials for cases of bottled water and self-heating meals and first-aid kits, like we're supposed to be preparing for the apocalypse. They're working on formulating laws for zombies, Mom says, so Dad comes home with more and more paperwork every night.

That's why I decided to try to get out of the house. If I can't avoid the zombie-influence on my life, I might as well prove I'm not afraid.

Mom picks us up at the movie theater, and Stella and I sit in the backseat together. Stella keeps pointing out things through the windows: restaurants she wants to try, the park where she broke her foot when she was a kid, houses that her cousin told her are haunted. She tells me some lie about how a kid in one of the apartment buildings is one-sixteenth yeti. "*So* furry," she says. "Like he's wrapped in a rug."

Then a minute later she says, "Look, Wil. Zombies."

I look. Mom pretends she's checking the traffic, but she looks, too.

"I don't know," I say. It's hard to tell. It's two grownups, just walking, not talking. I've seen a few people around who I think are zombies, but the only ones who are easy to identify are the kids. Little kid zombies are so creepy. The sit out on their lawns and stare, all hollowed out like pumpkins on Halloween. And they don't play with anything.

There's something way more wrong about the kid zombies than the adult ones. And now here I go thinking about Graham again, and all the reasons I need to get him back to normal. And all the things I've tried that he's ignored. Covering his room in pictures of the two of us fishing or camping with Mom and Dad. Throwing water balloons at him when he stepped outside to take out the trash. Stealing his toothbrush. Making him breakfast. I do mean things and I do nice things, and he says thank you and goes back to what he was doing.

And I'm beginning to think that what's going on inside our house is scarier than what's outside.

But I'm not giving up.

Stella looks at me and smiles, and I feel a little better.

WHEN I GET HOME, Graham is staring at the microwave while a bag of popcorn rotates on the turntable inside. "Hi," he says.

"Hi. You busy?"

"Hungry."

"Yeah. That's not the same thing."

He looks at me blankly, so I give him a big smile. "I was thinking I'd call Luke!" I say. He hasn't called since Graham blew him off last time. "You want to see Luke?"

Then we say, "I don't care," together. He seems confused that I saw that coming.

I decide to take that as an okay to call Luke. I tell him to bring Anthony. Apologizing in person will be easier. And getting Luke over is Plan D, or E, or something for getting Graham back to normal. Maybe he needs someone to talk to about football and girls and stupid stuff like that. If that's the first step to getting him closer to the real Graham, fine. He can start with the boring stuff. Then he can come back to me.

When Anthony gets here, we retreat to my room to give Graham and Luke some time. I want to spy on them, but when I suggest it, Anthony looks even angrier at me. If that's possible. "They give me the creeps," he says.

"Graham and Luke?"

"The zombies."

"Oh."

He glares at me.

We're sitting in my room, and he's picking at my curtains like someone's hired him to try to pull them apart. Like it's his job, and they're the only thing in this whole room that he cares about.

"I'm sorry," I say.

"I don't want to talk about it."

Great. Now what?

He's wearing this shirt that I know for a fact he hates, because one time my cat peed on the shirt he was wearing and his mom brought him that one to change into, and he complained for the rest of the day. His hair's bigger on one side than the other. I don't know what's up with him.

So I say, "Dude, are you okay?"

"I don't know how you're so calm about a zombie living in your house. You have no idea how dangerous zombies can be. We put my grandmother in a hotel immediately. *Immediately*."

"Bet that was your dad's idea."

"My dad's not here, okay? He left for a business trip the morning after they woke up. He didn't even say goodbye." I didn't know Anthony's glare could get any colder, but there it goes. "Because he has so much work to do because of what *you* did. And who knows when he's coming home because he hasn't called home *once* and my mom is *so scared* and it's all your fault!"

I kind of had a feeling that his dad wasn't around, because he hasn't been on the news calming people down. And a lot of the people on the political shows are yelling about why not. But it's still hard to hear it from Anthony, even though I know he doesn't like his dad.

"I'm sorry," I say again.

"You're going to be really sorry when Graham eats your brains when you're sleeping, okay? That's when you're really going to be sorry, because you were so stupid!"

"Come on. Graham isn't going to eat anyone's brains. He's just boring. He's not dangerous."

"Yeah, and all of a sudden you're the zombie expert."

That is so not fair. "I've *always* been the zombie expert!"

"And you're the one who taught us that zombies are dangerous! That you shouldn't believe anything they say to you because all they want to do is chew on your bones! That's what you said! And you should pay attention, okay, because just because he's your brother doesn't mean he's safe!"

But that's wrong. He's the world's lamest brother right now, but he's not dangerous. Why would he be? He doesn't care about anything.

So after a while I just say, "I'm sorry about your dad."

"I don't know why I let Luke force me to come here."

" 'Cause you want to play Zombie Tag?"

He looks up. Hopefully.

"Soon," I say. "Once Graham's well again. He'll play with us."

All of a sudden I'm in this memory. I'm waiting for Graham to stop wheezing so we can play another game

97

of hockey. And I'm so impatient, dying for Graham to quiet down and get up.

Anthony's voice brings me back. "I'm not crazy, you know? There are . . . lots of reasons to think the zombies might not be so safe."

Yeah. Even though none of the zombies—or the Re-instated Living, as the TV's calling them—have been violent or dangerous, the news has been pretty clear about saying that they're all walking around like empty shells, and any second they might snap and start shoplifting from our stores or blowing us up or something.

In total, I woke up seventy people. Which is not very many at all, if you think about it. And still people are already talking about what we're going to do in the fall, when school starts. Should we get separate classes for the zombies? What if they try to kill your children? Aaaaah.

I say, "They're just looking for something to talk about. They're totally taking advantage of the fact that nobody knows what happened with the zombies last time they woke up." The news keeps bringing up how they all died in that pile and no one knows why. Which means I keep listening at Graham's door at night to make sure he's still breathing.

We should really sell our TV.

Then Anthony clears his throat and goes, "Yeah. Nobody knows what happened last time."

I stare at him. Wait, what was that throat clearing? Why isn't Anthony looking at me?

What does he know that I don't know? *How?* I read *everything.*

Anthony shakes himself a little and stands up. "So are we going to spy on Luke and Graham, or what?"

I'll let him distract me, but I'm not forgetting what just happened.

We peek out of my doorway and into the living room. Graham and Luke are sitting on the couch together, but they're not talking. Luke is playing with his phone, and Graham's kind of staring into space.

Great. Thanks a lot, Luke.

"I can fix him," I whisper.

"Yeah." He has the bite back in his voice. " 'Cause you did such a good job with waking him up."

I look at him. "Hey."

I must have some sad expression on my face, because Anthony looks down and goes, "Sorry."

Then a minute later, he says, "I believe you, you know? That you can. That maybe there's a chance that he can . . . you know . . ." and then his voice gets really quiet and he says, "Love you."

Then he shakes his head really fast, and the collar of his ugly shirt is bobbing up and down while he swallows over and over. I say, "Dude, don't get weepy on me, okay?" What's going *on*?

"Sorry," he says. "Thinking about other stuff."

After a few minutes, Luke comes into the kitchen to get a soda, so we accost him. I say, "How does he look, Doctor?"

Luke shrugs his way into the fridge. "Hard to say. I see what you mean. He definitely seems a little less present than he did before. But . . . he could get on like this. He'd be okay."

"Yeah, I know he'd be okay." It's not like I thought the big bad world was going to eat him. "But do you think he could be Graham again?"

Luke says, "Aw, Wil, look at him."

I look. He's flipping through the channels, spending the exact same blank two seconds on each one before he changes to the next.

"He's Graham," Luke says. "He's just a little more . . . subdued."

"He's *numb*."

"Don't think of it as a big personality change, okay?" Luke pushes the tab on his soda can. "He's not a different person. He's just . . . I don't know, to be honest, he's a little ahead of the game in terms of adapting, don't you think?"

Anthony says, "What are you talking about?"

Luke crosses his arms. "Look, you always hear about how college or whatever will kill your innocence, right? Grow you up super-fast by putting your soul in the freezer. Graham's already ready for that. Adulthood's not going to slap him in the face, at least. That's a plus."

I shake my head.

"Just stop stressing, Wil!" Luke gives me a millisecond of a one-armed hug. "Your brother's back. You should be thrilled."

I know. "I know."

"And now I should be getting my brother back in time for dinner. Come on, Anthony."

Anthony stands up taller, but his voice gets younger, and he says, "Can we play Frisbee after dinner? If we get a hundred and twenty in a row, we'll break our old record."

"God, a hundred and twenty in a row? That's like half an hour."

Anthony lowers himself down. "So?"

"So . . . it's half an hour. I don't know. We'll see."

"Okay," Anthony says, all depressed. He and Luke shuffle toward the door. I give him my fist to tap on the way out, but he ignores it, so I guess maybe we're not okay. I thought we were.

Once the door shuts, I go and collapse next to Graham on the couch. "Hey, big guy. Big brother. Big Kahuna."

"Hey."

He looks really tired. But he's been sleeping so much. I hope he's not sick. I still don't know if he can get sick.

I say, "So did you have fun with Luke?"

"He's always been nice." Graham tugs at his sock. "I think I made him sad, though. He was frowning the way you do."

"He didn't seem sad when he was leaving."

"He talked about you." Graham looks right at me for what feels like the first time. My heart thrums at the exact same second his eyes lock on mine. It's eerie and terrifying.

Graham doesn't notice. "He talked about you," he says again. "Said that I need to be back to normal for you."

I find my voice. "I mean it's not a big deal or anything. I don't care. I don't even like you."

"You're telling a joke."

"Yeah."

"I thought so."

"So yeah, let's spend some time with little brother, fix his wounded soul." I flop backward on the couch. "You want to go over to the school? We can shoot baskets. You can be all normal."

He shrugs. "I'm kind of tired. Can I be all normal here?"

"Could you? Because that would make this all a lot simpler, I'll tell you that."

He's quiet when he says, "I feel fine, you know?"

"I know."

He's explained it. He doesn't feel weird. He doesn't feel like he's doing anything wrong. He doesn't feel anything.

Except tired, apparently.

I say, "Okay. I've got it. Let's go down to the creek. We can catch frogs."

"Why do we want frogs?"

"We'll let them go after. Catching them's the fun part. Like we used to every Sunday. Remember that?"

"Yeah. My brain isn't broken."

"Just your soul."

I was just kidding, but he says, "Yeah." Ugh. Graham. He thinks for a minute, then says, "We'll let them go?"

"Of course."

"Then what's the point?"

"It's . . . fun, Graham. It's what we always did. Just trust me, okay? I bet you'll like it."

He shrugs.

It's so quiet for so long, me just sitting here, staring at him.

I say, "Okay, well, will you ride your bike down there with me? I don't want to go alone." Once he's there, he won't be able to resist crawling into the mud and hunting for frogs. I know him. "If you're nice to me, maybe Luke will come over more. Wait, you don't care if Luke comes over more. God. *God*. How am I supposed to convince you to do anything?"

He shrugs.

"Just, please? Will you come?"

"I don't care."

Fine. "Okay, that means we're going. Come on."

Turns out, it's really useful that Mom kind of freaked out and refused to throw any of Graham's things away. He'd had enough clean clothes to last him all week, and his bike is ready to ride, except for some dust. I clean it off while he watches.

"Good as new," I say. "Just like you."

He raises his eyebrows, then he sneezes.

I strap on my helmet. "Let's go. Use your inhaler before we leave."

Usually, Graham and I race down to the creek, but today he rides slowly, so I do too, making sure I'm always right next to him. He doesn't turn his head to look at me, but the second he does, I'm going to be here. I'm ready when he is.

When we pedal past the shopping center, he picks up a hand to point straight ahead of us. "See them?" His voice is as calm and flat as the road.

I'm so excited that he started a conversation. I have to encourage it. "See what, Graham?" I push my voice as loud and strong as his isn't, making this big show out of being interested.

"Those are zombies."

They're the same ones Stella pointed out a few hours ago. I wonder if they've been walking this whole time.

I squint. "Yeah? How can you tell?"

"I don't know. Just can. Look at them when we get close."

By the time we get to them, they've sat down on a bench together. They're smoking cigarettes and staring into the distance, and they don't seem to notice Graham and me when we pass by.

"You see, yeah?" Graham says. "You can tell. They didn't really seem interested in anything. They're just kind of here."

I say, "They didn't look any different from real adults."

"Yeah?" He shrugs. "Whatever."

We weave through a line of laughing kids waiting in line for the ice-cream truck.

I lead Graham to this particular part of the creek, where there's a fallen tree lying across the fifteen feet between the banks. It's the closest the creek has had to a bridge since the real thing finally rotted away years ago. The creek is right behind our synagogue, and Graham and I used to sneak out here instead of going to Hebrew school.

I throw my bike down in the mud and run over to the log. "Graham, remember that time I fell off?"

"Yeah." He has his arms crossed, and he stays on the bank like he's afraid to get dirty.

"Remember? I'll tell you about it so you'll remember."

"Wil, I remember."

106

But he doesn't *really*. You can't remember something like that with your arms crossed. He can't remember it and not want to tell the story at the same time as me, our versions of it overlapping and arguing, the same way they have at every family reunion ever.

I say, "I was just worried about getting caught in my dirty clothes, but you saw that my foot was caught under that big rock, remember?"

"Yeah. I knew you'd break your ankle if you kept struggling."

"So you dove into the water—all the way in!—and you got the rock off my foot. Remember?"

"Yeah, Wil."

"You were totally my hero that day. That's so lame to say, but you totally, totally were." I look up at him with my biggest smile, the kind I used to give when he had a toy I wanted to play with. It's not real, because I'm not happy, but it wasn't real when I was trying to get something from him, either, and it always worked then.

Now Graham looks away and sighs. "Are you going to play, or what?"

I stare at him for a minute, then I climb back onto the bank and pinch him, hard.

"Ow." He pulls his arm away and looks at it like it confused him.

I do it again.

"That hurts."

"So tell me to stop!"

He says, "Stop," like he's ordering off a menu.

"No. Yell at me!"

He keeps watching me, his eyebrows bunched together. "Why?"

"Because I'm hurting you!" And then my hands are around his neck. My fingers are wrapping around it. I'm not squeezing, but I could. I could make him stop breathing right now. He isn't fighting. He isn't trying to pull away. "Because I'm going to keep hurting you until you yell at me." I put all my weight on one of his feet. "Do something. Yell at me."

He doesn't yell at me. I give up. I let go of his neck and step off his foot.

It's harder to stop than I thought it would be.

That story about the creek isn't my favorite time that Graham saved me, not even close. I remember the one that's really my favorite that night, while Jack Bandit is snoring on top of my face, and I'm trying to think of a better way to bring Graham back. Ways that will leave me less angry and him less bruised.

It was, like, exactly a year ago, only a few months before Graham died. I was at Anthony's birthday party at the roller skating rink, and he invited Eben, which I thought was so stupid. I guess it made sense, because Eben's parents are friends with Anthony's parents, but that didn't mean Anthony needed to act like Eben was his best friend the whole time, and he totally did. We barely even knew Eben then. It's not like he lived next door.

Anthony's parents gave him these amazing roller-blades before the party. The wheels were thin and smooth so he could skate faster than everyone. I asked if I could try them, since I was in worn-out hand-me-down skates. He said no. I just wanted to try them on for one lap around the rink, and he shot me completely down. So, whatever. I didn't cry about it or anything. It's a pair of skates.

But the next thing I know I turn around and Eben's wearing the skates! And Anthony let him keep them on for, like, fifteen minutes. I only wanted them for one lap.

I guess it sounds stupid, but I didn't want to be at the party after that. But if I told his parents, it would have been a big deal and they'd have made me feel awful for getting mad at Anthony on his birthday. I didn't want to cause a scene or give Mr. Lohen an excuse to rip me to pieces. I just wanted to get out of there because I felt so upset and stupid.

So I went into the gross roller rink bathroom to call my parents, hoping they'd pick me up quietly and I could pretend I had a stomachache or something. I called my house, and Graham picked up. "They're across the street," he said. "Having a very lovely impromptu dinner party with the Gershwins. La di da, aren't we so fancy." The Gershwins are the ones who uninvited them this week.

"Can you go get them?" I said.

"Wil, you okay? Your voice sounds funny."

"I don't think I'm Anthony's best friend anymore and I just don't want to be here and I know it's stupid but my skates suck and I want to come home, okay?"

I expected him to laugh at me, or, if I was really lucky, for him to say, "Okay, I'll go get Mom and make her call you."

But instead he said, "Don't even worry about it, okay?

It's going to be fine. Play cool for a little while and I'll be right there."

It actually took almost an hour, because Graham had to bike all the way across town. By the time he got there, the party was practically over, but I was still totally fuming.

He walked through the rink doors like a cowboy into a saloon. His sweaty helmet was hanging off his arm. "Hey, champ. Ready to jump ship?"

"Let's just sneak out, okay?"

He laughed. "Nah, man. Do you want to face the Lohens after that? Hold on just a sec." He put his arm around me and walked me over to the Lohens and smiled and shook hands. Mr. Lohen was glaring at him so hard. He probably hated Graham more than he hated anyone, which is a pretty big honor for my brother, I guess.

Graham said, "Hey, I'm really sorry, but my mom's iguana just died, and she wants to have us all home right now."

Mrs. Lohen frowned. "Oh, dear. I had no idea your mother had an iguana."

"Yeah, he's like—or, he was like, I guess—a part of the family. Wellington." Graham took a few of these big breaths, and I swear he faked his way all the way to teary eyes. "I'm sorry, this is so difficult. He was so young and spry."

Mrs. Lohen offered him a tissue, and Graham nodded gratefully while he patted my shoulder and I tried to look mournful.

He dabbed at his cheek. "I really think we should be with our mother to help her through this."

"That sounds best." Mrs. Lohen took the tissue back and folded it into a little square, which was really weird.

Graham said, "Mom's going to be pretty heartbroken about this for a while, I think. You might not want to mention it to her."

"Oh, of course not."

"We should get going. Thanks for surrendering Wil. We won't forget your kindness to us during this awful time." And with that, Graham led me out of the roller rink, and nobody ever asked me about it.

Outside, he gave me a hug but didn't say anything.

I was kind of uncomfortable with the hug. It's not that I minded it, really, it just felt like a weird time, and *anyone* could see it. But I owed him, so I nodded and said, "Thanks."

"You don't need Anthony," he said, and I rode on his handlebars all the way home.

And of course the next day Anthony told me that his parents had forced him to be nice to Eben because his mom was in the hospital with phlebitis. So everything was okay. Even though Graham and I went back to arguing and stealing socks and hiding each other's toothbrushes in the litter box, I didn't forget that Graham didn't think I needed a best friend, because either it meant he thought I was cool enough to handle everything alone or—and this was what I hoped—it meant that he was really my best friend, quietly, forever, no matter what.

I mean, after all, whose skates had I been wearing? Graham's, of course.

DAD COMES HOME about three hours late from work tonight. My mom's mad because dinner's cold, and then she's mad that she's acting like the kind of mother who sits and frets about dinner being cold, so she takes it out on me and the state of my room. By the time Dad comes home, I feel like I've been locked in my room performing manual labor for the last million years, and I just want to collapse into a plate of mashed potatoes and chicken. No drama. No weird zombie stuff. Just us and some meaningless conversation and some cold food.

And then I find out that Dad's in a worse mood than Mom is, and it's not like Graham's going to chat us all up and cool everyone down, so it looks like we're gearing up for the worst dinner ever.

I guess Dad has a good reason to be all worn-out and harried. The zombie who had his job last is trying to get it back, and his boss might be caving in fear of the old guy's zombie-wrath.

I'd be lying if I said I didn't feel pretty bad about this.

Dad scrapes a mouthful of potatoes off his plate. "I swear, anyone who's worked for the company since its inception thinks he can just waltz in and start working exactly where he left off."

Mom says, "Well, it's almost nice, if you think about it. They come back from the dead, and they just want to do their jobs and live like they used to. It's a little cute." I think she's trying to squelch her own bad mood so the whole table doesn't burst into angry flames. Although that would heat the food back up. My chicken is like rubber bands right now.

Dad says, "Maybe if they had any passion for their jobs whatsoever. But they just want to work because it's what they're used to. They aren't invested in the company."

It's not as if Dad goes off to work whistling in the morning, but whatever.

He says, "And half of them have never seen a computer before. Now, before you say anything, you know I'm the biggest advocate for zombie rights of anyone in the company . . ."

Mom ignores him, because we've all heard this speech a million times in the past two weeks. Dad's been preaching the rights of zombies to anyone who will listen. Which isn't much of anybody since everyone thinks we're crazy for even letting Graham live in the house with us.

Graham is chewing his chicken really deliberately, rolling his teeth around to grind it into pieces.

Mom says, "I'm sure it must feel nice to go back to something familiar. I bet Graham's excited to get back into his real life." She beams at him across the table.

He keeps chewing.

I say, "He doesn't even care."

Mom and Dad look at me, then they turn and look at each other.

I think they liked that I was still holding out hope. It meant they didn't have to worry about it. But now I'm starting to waver and they look scared.

Or maybe they're just grateful that their son stopped being the idiot who expects his zombie brother to suddenly go back to normal. God. Am I that idiot?

Then Dad gives me this stretched smile and chuckles. "He's a teenager. What do you expect?"

Mom says, "I would have been pretty surprised if he were jumping for joy at going back to school in

September. Bet you thought you were done with that forever, huh?"

Yeah, I'm sure in Graham's last breathless, terrifying seconds, he was thanking his lucky stars that he wouldn't have to go back to high school. Give me a break.

Huh.

Maybe that's what this all is. Maybe Graham's a mess because of how scary his death was. If Graham had survived the asthma attack, we wouldn't have expected him to be normal immediately after. He'd be freaked that he'd had such a bad attack, and we'd be totally worried about him, and we'd all need some time before we got back to normal.

But we never got to do that. Especially not Graham. So maybe it's like he's been asleep for a long time, and now he's awake and facing all those feelings, and he's scared.

I watch Graham. He licks his fork.

I can't tell if he's scared. He could be. I try not to think about how easy it used to be to know exactly what was in Graham's head.

"You okay?" I ask him, quietly, once Mom has Dad distracted talking about this thing she's thinking about doing with her hair.

Graham says, "What?"

It's scary now when he looks at me. There's something just so wrong about the expression on his face, like it's threatening to lose interest in me any second. I feel like I need to fight to keep him looking at me, to realize that I'm actually here and that should matter to him.

Look at me.

I feel like he really saw me that time on the couch yesterday. I feel like we were actually getting somewhere.

I feel like I was wrong.

I say, "I said are you okay?"

He looks at his hands, like he's checking for cuts. And he takes a few breaths in and out, testing. "Don't I look okay?"

"You look kind of sad, I guess." He doesn't really, but this seems like a good place to start.

"Oh." Graham turns back to his food. "I don't feel sad."

"Then how do you feel?"

I regret those words as soon as they're out of me. Because I know exactly what he's going to say, and I don't want to hear it. And I don't know why I keep expecting something different.

118

"Wil." He puts down his fork loudly enough for Mom and Dad to look at us. "I don't feel anything," he says. "I'm not saying this to make you mad. I'm not trying to crush your dreams. I have no interest in hurting you whatsoever. I have no interest in *anything*. I don't care about what anybody's talking about, and I don't care that I don't care." He shrugs and takes another bite. "I guess this chicken is good."

Mom says, "Thank you, Graham."

I can't believe this is happening. How can Mom talk to him like everything's normal? "I can fix you," I say. "I can figure it out."

"I'm not a problem. I don't care if you fix me."

"But you will once you're fixed."

"Whatever."

"I'm going to make everything just how it was," I say, softly.

And then I'll get rid of this feeling in my stomach that's still telling me I made a horrible mistake waking up the dead. And I'll ride on his handlebars. And I'll teach all the dead people how to be normal. I'll be king of the zombies for real. "I'm going to fix you," I say. "And then you'll thank me forever. For*ever*."

"Okay, Wil. Fine."

119

I look at Mom and Dad, but they just shrug. "You know how teenagers are," Mom says, quietly.

I can't believe she's making it sound like it's normal or acceptable for people to just lose their feelings. This isn't okay.

And not to mention that even if it were, Graham and I spit on our hands and promised we would never, ever grow up. He's not going to get out of that just by dying.

I'm in my room, trying to find all the stuff I lost in the Great Clean-Up of 6 p.m., when Graham knocks on my open door. "Hey," he says.

I won't look up. "What do you want?"

"To talk to you." He comes in and flops down on the bed. For a minute, it's like we're back in time, and he's coming in here to complain about a test he has coming up or this girl who said she'd call back and then didn't. And I'd pretend to listen while I lay on the floor and rolled a baseball from hand to hand, wondering when he was going to shut up so we could go play.

"Can we talk?" he says.

Even though I don't mean to, I nod really hard.

"Because I know you don't understand this. And that . . . isn't fair to you."

I keep nodding. "I want to understand."

Graham takes a minute, then he tips his head up toward the ceiling. "Okay. So after I died, at the beginning . . . it was terrifying, you know?"

Terrified. That's a feeling. I'm clinging to it like it's my pillow after a nightmare.

He says, "It's lonely, and it's scary, and it's different, and there's no one to talk to, and all I wanted to do was come home. It was all I could think about ever. How much I missed Mom and Dad and you and my friends. Like, you've never wanted anything as much as I wanted to come back those first few days. It rips you into pieces. You're desperate to move, to scream, to breathe, to find some way."

I say, "But now you're home."

"After those first few days, though . . ." Graham shakes his head. "It all goes away. You stop caring. I . . . I was feeling way too much. I couldn't keep going that way. Not when I knew there was no way I was coming back."

"You *did* come back."

"But I was so sure I wasn't going to. So I had to let it all go." He makes eye contact with me. "I'm not like this to make you feel bad. And I really . . ." It's like he can't remember the word he wants. "I appreciate that you want to help me."

No. No. We're having a conversation. He's talking to me. We're too close to normal to give up now. I say, "Look. I know we can get you back. Because you chose to lose your feelings, right? You're lying there, you're dead and alone, and you turn off. You chose to do it."

He thinks about it. "I knew it had to happen at some point, no matter if I fought. But, yeah."

"So you can choose to get them back."

"No, Wil. I don't think it's possible. I have no reason to believe there's any way to go back to who I was. And neither do you."

A thought throbs my chest.

I bet the answer is in that notebook.

I slap my pockets immediately, even though these are different jeans than the pair I was wearing. I think back to taking the shards of the bell out of my pocket, carefully placing each and every one into a plastic bag in my desk. I would have put the notebook away, too, if I had it.

I must have dropped it when I fell at Anthony's, the same moment I broke the bell.

But where is it now?

I shake my head and come back to Graham. "If you really want to get your feelings back, I know we can . . ."

"I don't want to," he says.

I stare at him. "What?"

"I don't want to feel anything anymore."

"Why? Because you're *scared?*"

"Scared is a feeling," he says, softly. Patiently.

"Okay, because it's scary? Because you think you *would* be scared?"

"Well . . . yes."

"You can't just be nothing forever because you're scared!"

He says, "But, see . . . yeah, I can. I'm sorry, but I really can."

Maybe he's just pretending that he doesn't have feelings, because it's easier.

Maybe it's way easier not to love me.

GOING TO THE MALL to see *Tornadoes of Doom* again is kind of stupid, since I didn't like it much the first time, but at least it gets me out of the house. And Anthony's here, which should be cool, but he's quiet while we're all walking through the mall, like he thinks we're still in the theater. And he's wearing his backpack from school. It's *summer.*

Stella's throwing leftover popcorn pieces in the air as we walk and trying to catch them in her mouth, and David's yanking on her braids so she either misses or chokes every time. Eben is twitchy and nervous about it, unsurprisingly, worried a piece is going to get lodged her throat. I really hope he doesn't have a thing for Stella. That would be so gross. And so not okay with me. As her friend.

"Did you like the movie?" I ask Anthony, because he's just so quiet.

"It was fine. Look . . ." He takes a deep breath. "We should probably talk."

I widen my eyes and go, "Are you breaking up with me?"

David laughs, and Stella says, "Aw, Wil's smiling."

I say, "What?"

"You've been a pouty little mess all day."

"Really?"

They all kind of nod at me. Oh. Maybe that's why Anthony wanted to talk. Wanted to make sure I wasn't about to throw myself down the escalator or something. "Yeah, I don't know, I guess I'm . . . I guess I gave up on Graham."

"I need to talk to you," Anthony says, but now I'm thinking about Graham.

David frowns. "Why are you giving up?"

"He doesn't want to be normal and I don't know how to get him back to normal. So I'm cutting my losses. No more brother for me. Snip."

I'm trying to joke about it, but even I can tell what a drip I sound like.

"Look," I say. "I'm done moping. Done. Time to move on."

Stella grabs me by my chin and looks at me. "Except you're still moping."

125

Her fingers are sticky from all the sour straws we ate. I pull away. "I'll get over it."

David says, "You shouldn't have to get over it. He came back. Do you know how lucky you are for that?"

Anthony's tugging on my sleeve again. Anthony, Christ. I'm not here, leave a message. David and I are sharing a dead family moment right now.

And David's staring at me, and I don't know how to tell him *but he's not really back* without sounding like a total jerk.

"Luke ignores Anthony sometimes, too," Eben says.

Eben is the worst. He's just the worst ever. I say, "Yeah, that isn't the same."

"Why, because he's *your* brother?"

"Because my brother's a *zombie*." I guess I say this kind of loudly, because people around us all glance at me and then quickly look away. Except for this security guard, whose eyes get stuck on me.

I hate the mall. We came here to see the movie only because Eben said these girls from his class that he liked were talking online last night about going here. Eben is so creepy. I can't believe he stalks the girls in his class online. They're not worth stalking. They're too tall and built like sticks. Most of them, anyway. I guess there's Mary. And Stella.

It's not like we're here to see eighth graders or something. Those are the girls worth looking at.

"Let's check the food court," Eben says. "Myra said they were going to get cheese fries. She told Jen to meet her next to the trash cans."

Creepy. Creepy. So much stalking. I say, "Okay. Whatever. I don't care."

He laughs in his throat. "You sound like Graham."

Anthony says, "Shut *up*, Eben. You guys need to stop *joking* about this."

I look at him. His teeth are clenched and his shoulders are shaking when he breathes. Seriously, what is going on with him?

But then I say, "Anthony," and he says, "Not now." I thought he wanted to talk to me.

Fine. I don't have time for his drama anyway. I have plenty of my own. And whatever's up with him is his issue, not mine.

That security guard is following me. There are so many more around than there used to be. They're lurking outside the stores and by the piercing booths and the ice-cream stands.

Besides that, the mall doesn't seem that much different from how it did before. I guess most of the zombies are too old to hang out at the mall on a Saturday. It's not like our cemetery was stuffed with sixteen-year-olds.

I see a few people who walk around like a part of them is missing, but I can't tell if they're zombies or that's who they are normally. I can't ever understand adults, and throwing zombies into the mix hasn't helped at all.

A bunch of eighth-graders—definitely not zombies—rush by us on skateboards and nearly knock us down. They're going to get in so much trouble, but, God, how cool would it be to ride a skateboard through the mall? I wonder if I'll be like that in a year. That's the kind of teenager I want to be. I'm brave enough to do it; I really am.

One of the security guards—sadly, not the one trailing me—sprints after him.

"There are a ton of guards around," I say.

Anthony mumbles, "Dad says theft's highest in summer."

"Oh." This is the first time I've heard Anthony mention his dad since he left for his endless business trip. I asked Luke last time he was over to see Graham, and he said no one's heard from him. Luke didn't seem all that concerned.

Anthony says, "Blood boils. People steal stuff." He pauses. "Like his bell."

I hiss air out between my teeth. God, Anthony. Does he have to bring that up every time I see him?

David says, "Hey!" He tugs on my elbow until I stop. "I want to see if they have that alien game, the one Kyle has."

"You couldn't even afford it," Stella says.

"Shut up. You don't know me." That's weird. Graham used to say that all the time. I guess David got that from me.

David starts to go inside, but my security guard steps over and blocks his way. David sticks his hands in the pockets of his shorts. "What?"

"I don't think so, son." But he's looking at me.

David says, "Are you kidding me? I didn't do anything. I haven't even gone inside. You totally can't arrest me."

The security guard laughs. It's short and hard like a cough. "You're not under arrest. We just think it'd be best if you took your business elsewhere."

"He can afford the game, probably," Anthony says. "We were just playing around."

Eben says, "Guys, maybe we should just go."

I shrug a little. Stella told me the other day that I should be careful around cops, that they could be dangerous and violent because all the ones who died on duty are back without their badges but maybe with their uniforms and their appetite for revenge. This doesn't sound legit to me, since I'm pretty sure "bloodthirsty" is a feeling. Also, I don't think mall security guards really count as cops.

The security guard points to a small sign taped to the shop window: NO ZOMBIES.

Anthony says, "Whoa, we're not zombies!"

"You were just talking about them," the security guard says. "I heard you."

"Yeah, *talking* about them."

I say, "We don't even look like zombies. We're kids."

"I've seen kid zombies."

I give up. I can't prove that I'm not a zombie, and I really can't prove that zombies aren't any threat to this store. Especially since I'm beginning to suspect that I don't know anything at all about zombies. After all, what kind of zombie master couldn't really bring back his own brother?

"Come on," I tell David. "We'll get the game

somewhere else. You can buy it online. No stupid security guards there."

The security guard glares at me.

David stalks away with us, his arms crossed. "I can't believe this."

"It's not a big deal. Come on. Let's go find those girls so Eben will stop whining."

"I'm not whining!"

When we get to the food court, the girls aren't there. That's okay. A slice of pizza and a soda cools David off, even though Eben's still sulking.

"You want to come to my house tonight?" David asks us. "My sister rented this movie. We can steal it from her room. It's rated R for nudity."

Stella says she's in. Eben is too. Anthony just shrugs. "I can't tonight," I say.

"Why not?"

"Graham . . ." But I don't know if this is the real reason, or if I'm just touchy because of drippy Anthony.

And Anthony laughs a little without looking at me, not in a good way. "This is exactly like what you used to do. 'I can't play, I have to tag along after Graham.'"

I slam my empty cup on the counter. "What is your problem?"

He looks at me for a long time before he says anything. "You should just let this thing with Graham go, okay? You made a horrible mistake waking up the zombies, and who even knows who could have been hurt, and you don't even know what zombies are like and you didn't know what you were doing and now you're blowing us all off to hang out with some dried-up dead boy who doesn't even want you!"

No one says anything. Stella takes a really loud sip of her soda.

Eventually David says, "Dude, take a walk or something."

"Yeah." Anthony throws his backpack at the corner of our booth and stands up. "Yeah, I'll take a walk." He lopes away with his hands in his pockets.

"What is *up* with him?" David says.

Stella looks at me while she munches her way down a french fry. "Wil, you okay?"

"Fine." I'm staring at the backpack Anthony left, and the blue notebook that's peeking through the open zipper.

I know that notebook.

He's had it this whole time.

I curl my hands into fists.

I wait until my friends get distracted throwing food at each other, then I start balling up napkins and wrappers so it looks like I'm just cleaning up. When I get close to Anthony's backpack, I grab the notebook and stash it in my pocket. My heart's beating so hard it feels like it's shaking.

This is what I need. This is my only hope. As soon as I get to the trash can, I open it.

The notebook naturally falls open to one of the heaviest pages near the back. This section is all newspaper articles, clipped and glued like an art project from fourth grade. Some of them are from the past few years—ZOMBIE FEAR RE-EMERGING, GOVERNMENT INSTABILITY TO BLAME? and ON THE 30TH ANNIVERSARY, VISIONS OF A (PERHAPS?) ZOMBIELESS FUTURE—but most of the articles are yellow and faded and dated thirty-two years ago.

PILE OF DEAD IN MOSQUITO LAKE, ALASKA; WERE THOSE ZOMBIES IN ALASKA, AND COULD WASHINGTON, D.C. BE NEXT? and HOW TO PREPARE YOURSELF FOR ZOMBIE WARFARE.

I hurry back to the beginning of the notebook, before the newspaper articles start. Here, it's all handwritten, like a journal, except the words are all over the place and it's hard to follow.

Back. Not really back. Physically here but it's like I'm somewhere else. Keeping a record. If something happens, here's a record. Here it is. I was alive and I'm alive again. Maybe someday I'll care enough to reread this entry.

Whoa.

It's a diary. It's a zombie diary.

Over at the booth, Stella screams because David's stuffing ice down her back, and thank God this breaks my concentration long enough for me to see that Anthony's headed back from the bathroom and walking straight toward us.

So I do something that's probably pretty stupid.

I rip a handful of pages out of the front of the notebook before I slip it back into Anthony's backpack.

One time when we were camping in our backyard, Graham said, "What do you think happens when you die?"

We used to do that sometimes. Lug our sleeping bags out and pitch our tent and lie out there, pretending we had a campfire. We couldn't do it too much because Graham would usually start wheezing from lying in the grass all night, but I loved it, and I was always pushing him to do it more often, which made Mom mad.

It was really late, but so loud from the frogs and the cicadas.

I said, "I don't . . . think about stuff like that."

"Everyone thinks about stuff like that."

"Yeah, okay, but I don't think you're supposed to discuss it, you know? You're supposed to think about it quietly to yourself."

"Talking to you is like talking to myself."

I hoped he didn't see me smile at that, because it didn't sound like a compliment, even though it felt like one. I think it was too dark for him to see, anyway.

He rolled over, and the grass crunched under him while he coughed. I stretched out. I was thinking about how good a s'more would taste right then.

He said, "Okay, so you die, and just . . . things keep happening without you?"

"Yeah."

"That doesn't make sense."

"Um . . . I think most people agree on that one."

"But, like, how? Like . . ." He was quiet here for a

135

long time. "Like I was just coughing, and then I stopped coughing, and everything was the same as it was before I started."

"Yeah."

"But coughing isn't *dying*. How can dying just be a thing?" He shook his head. "I don't know, Wil. I don't know. I don't think things will go on without me."

I laughed. "I can't believe how self-centered you are."

"It's the curse of being the person the world revolves around. A blessing and a curse."

"You're a drip."

He said, "But seriously. No one can say for sure that the world keeps going after they die. Because how would you know? Maybe you're the one who the world can't exist without. I mean, there has to be *someone*, right? One person dies and the universe is like, that's it, straw that broke the camel's back, I'm done, peace, there's no point in doing this anymore if people are going to keep keeling over on me."

"That's so stupid." I rolled over on the grass and looked at him. "Billions of people have already died, and here we are."

"But it takes only one person."

"And that person's going to be you?"

"Hey, you don't know me." He laughed. His breathing was getting noisy.

I said, "Of course I know you. That's the point."

"Yeah." His breath caught, and he coughed some more. "You're pretty lucky to know me, let's be honest."

AS SOON AS I'M HOME, once I've assured the parents I
didn't die in David's mom's junky car and said hi to the
listless brother on my couch, I sit on the floor of my
room and unfold the notebook pages from my pocket.

This is the second time I've stolen from Anthony in
the past two weeks. I'm the world's worst friend.

But it's not like he gets a gold star in friendship, either, since he hadn't mentioned this notebook to me.

When I was young and obsessed with dragons, I had
a notebook like this. I used to cut out newspaper articles
that mentioned dragons and glue them onto the pages,
back when dragons were still cool. I called it my case file.
I hope Eben never finds about that. He'd use it against
me somehow.

I guess this is the same sort of thing as my case file. If

Mr. Lohen's department had the bell, it makes sense they'd have the last remaining zombie evidence, too. God, some dads just have the coolest jobs.

Jack Bandit curls up against my knee, and I start reading from where I left off. I should have stolen more pages.

Am trying to acclimate to real life, but we are not going back to our human homes. We see no reason to. We know what they would do to us. We hide together. It is cold. The only thing in the world is cold.

I'm scanning every word, waiting for the one that will be magic for bringing back the real Graham.

Ate oatmeal. It tasted like oatmeal.

But to be honest, this stuff is kind of tedious.

And that isn't changing as I keep reading. The pages I have are nothing but day by day accounts of having no feelings. And it's hard to care because he doesn't care, and because this zombie isn't my brother. And because I've seen so much of this lately that reading about it is about as fun as a headache.

Not to mention, I keep getting distracted by this weird, kind of snuffly noise that sounds like it's coming from down the hall. I can't figure out what it is. It sounds like an animal's gotten into the house, but Jack Bandit doesn't seem concerned, and last time we had a mouse, he hid on top of my bookshelf and cried until we chased it back outside.

Crying. That's what this is. Someone's crying.

If it were Dad, I wouldn't worry, because Dad cries all the time, though he'd kill me if he thought I knew that. This is Mom. I can tell by the little whinnies at the end of every sob. She makes noises like a horse when she laughs, too.

It's making it so hard to concentrate. I don't have time to worry about Mom crying. God, I'm trying to fix what she's crying about, here. I wrap my arm around my head to cover my ears.

Graham Graham Graham Graham. Focus on Graham.

The zombie who wrote this journal didn't date his entries. If he weren't already dead, twice, I swear I'd kill him for that. I want to know how long he was alive the second time. If Graham's about to spontaneously die like those other zombies, if our zombies are about to throw themselves into a pile and die again, I'd like to know how long from now that's going to be. Some advance warning would be nice, this time.

Eventually, I hit an entry that just says: *The others*

want something from me that I can't give them, and it's making me so mad.

I stop and stare at the paper.

It's making me so mad.

Then I'm at Graham's door, pounding as hard as I can. "Let me in!"

From inside, he sighs. "Wil . . ."

I keep banging on the door. I know how this works. Thirty seconds of knocking, and he has to open the door.

And he does. "God, Wil, what?"

"Listen to me."

He holds up his hand. "No, you know what?" He breathes out hard and shoves his hand against his forehead. "Wil, I'm getting tired of this, okay? No more stupid plans to get me back to how I was. There isn't any going back. Accept it. I have. And just . . ." He's breathing slow to try to keep his voice down, but it isn't working. "Just *leave me alone, okay?*"

"Listen to you!"

"Listen to *what*, Wil?"

"You're mad at me!"

"*Because you're being an idiot.*"

I shove the notebook pages right in his face. "Mad," I say, "is a *feeling*."

Graham stares at the page, his shoulders still heaving up and down with every loud breath. Then he snatches the notebook out of my hand. I see his eyes tracing the words over and over again.

"What is this?" he says.

"Forget that." I stuff the pages in my pocket. "Look at me."

He does. He has his lip between his teeth, and all of a sudden he looks really young.

I whisper, "Come back."

"I . . ."

"You can't be scared. Scared is a feeling you don't have. It's just mad. It starts with mad. Mad comes first."

"How do you know?"

"Start with mad, and we'll work from there. *Work with me.*" I reach out and grab his fingers. I hold them all in my palm so they can't get away.

Graham slowly starts to nod, then he keeps going, faster and faster. "Yeah. Okay. Let's try it."

WE WANT MORE than anger, so we try a few feelings, just to see.

We start with happy. I take him on walks outside and surprise him with a sleepy cat on his stomach. I make nachos. I give him socks straight out of the dryer. He looks at me and shrugs.

So we try sad. We watch *Old Yeller*, and he sits there with his face still the whole time. The old Graham used to cry at movies. Not just sad movies, either. Comedies. Action movies. Horror movies. I teased him for that so much. Now, I get nothing.

"The only thing I've felt so far is anger," Graham says. We're in his room, flopped over the bed and the chair, working on a new plan. Graham seems even more bored than usual. He better not try to give up.

I say, "Maybe once it's strong enough, something else comes. You need to push through the anger and get to something else."

He nods a little. "Maybe." He shakes himself a little and stands up. "Okay. Make me mad."

"You're ugly and I hate you."

"Wil. Come on. Put some effort into it." He has his eyes squeezed shut in concentration. I stand up, too, and I look around the room like my race car posters are going to give me ideas.

I can't remember how I used to make him mad. It would happen so quickly that I wouldn't even know I'd messed up until he had me in a half-nelson.

So I say the first thing I can think of. "I'm mad at you for dying."

He opens his eyes. "What?"

"You left me here all alone to take care of Mom and Dad. And they were so messed up. They're still so messed up. And the counselor at school made me come in and talk to her. And she smelled funny and she wasn't even nice."

He rolls his eyes.

"Don't do that! Dad won't drive more than five miles over the speed limit, okay, and he's convinced someone's going to jump out and shoot us whenever we're in the city. We didn't even think about this stuff before you died. You put all these *ideas* in our heads. Now everyone thinks they're going to die all the time because of you."

Graham watches me. For a second I think this isn't working, then I see one of his hands curl into a fist.

I keep going, because at this point I don't think I can stop. "You shouldn't have died. You shouldn't have let the attack get that bad."

"You think I meant for that to happen?"

"You should have had your inhaler."

"I was *looking* for it."

"You should have known where it was! You should have found it faster!"

He takes a step toward me. "Let's see you do this, okay? Let's give *you* asthma and see you be the perfect little patient. *It's not that easy*." His teeth are all tight and his voice sounds more like Dad's than it ever has.

He has no idea how many nights I lay awake figuring out exactly how he could have breathed. Exactly what he should have done. How I would have done it.

I would have kept breathing.

"I did everything I could," he says. "Everything. I

fought and I fought and I looked and I tried to scream and *nobody was home . . .*"

No. There has to have been a way. There was a way he could have lived. He didn't have to die. I've grabbed onto this thought since his funeral and I'm wrapping my arms around it and I'm not letting it go. Graham was never supposed to die.

So I narrow my eyes at him and say, "You could have breathed if you cared enough."

"*I cared so much*!" he shouts, and then his hands hit my chest and I hit the floor.

Hard.

He's on top of me, driving punches into my stomach, grunting curses at me and keeping me down with all his weight. He's screaming, "You don't know *anything*! You were at *Anthony's*!"

I close my eyes and try to wait it out. At some point, he'll let me go. He always does. This is so familiar that it almost doesn't hurt.

Except it does.

"Let me up, Graham," I manage to say.

He responds with another punch in my gut. My stomach crashes like my organs are running into each other.

146

"*God*! Come on, man, let me up!"

I need him off of me. This isn't fun anymore.

I kick my feet as hard as I can, and I grab the carpet to try to pull myself away, but I can't. He's still so much stronger than I am. It's getting harder to catch my breath between punches.

I have to get out.

I hit him on top of his head—the zombie paralysis move—but it doesn't work. I can't believe part of me is surprised.

He hits me again. Oh, God. I can't take this anymore. Oh God Oh God Oh God *stop*.

I get my feet up and kick him hard with both feet, like a rabbit, square in his chest. The shock of it pushes him off me and across the floor. "*Off me!*" I shout.

He stares at me. He looks wild, and I think for a minute he's going to come at me again. But he doesn't.

I wrap my arms around my stomach and breathe. Everything hurts.

I can't believe he did that. I'm going to have huge bruises. He should have quit a long time ago. He should have fought fair.

I bet he's scared I'm going to tell Mom and Dad. They used to ground him if he hit me too hard. But he never

hit me like that. He should have stopped. I wasn't playing anymore.

Then he stands up and starts pacing. He has one hand
tight against his forehead, and he's groaning with his
exhales. And he's shaking.

And then he's taking these little steps toward me and
forcing himself back. I hear him mumbling, "Don't do it,
don't do it." He's holding his fist into himself like it's the
only way he can keep it from swinging, while he rubs his
teeth against each other.

He wasn't playing either.

But I know he won't hurt me. I know it deep inside me.
Somewhere.

I'm terrified.

"We have to stop this," he says. His voice doesn't
sound right.

But I say, "No." Ow. I close my eyes so he won't see
me wince. "We're getting somewhere."

"Somewhere I don't want to get. And . . . you don't
want to get there either." He looks at me. "I'm going to
hurt you if we keep doing this."

"You'd never really hurt me."

"God, *shut up*! Look. We're done here. This is over."

"Don't do this."

"*GET OUT OF MY ROOM!*" he shouts, and I'm up even though it hurts to stand and I'm out of the room so fast because I'm afraid he's going to start hitting me again.

And the voice inside my head saying, "Give up," is getting louder and louder.

And it's adding, "And run. *Run.*"

THAT NIGHT, IT'S ME in the bathroom, scared, suffocated. The door's locked, and I need to find Graham because Graham is the Key, but every time I open a drawer, I just find bits of him. His eye, half his nose, one of his hands. I need to find the whole Graham, but I don't think he's here, and the zombies are going to eat my lungs and I'll die locked in here and I'll die alone and I'm so dizzy and I can't breathe. . . .

And I wake up and throw my pillow off my face and start to cry.

My shirt is soaked with sweat, and my chest is pounding so hard it hurts. I'm afraid I'm going to have a heart attack. After a nightmare, I'm afraid of everything. My ceiling fan sounds like it has teeth. The crickets sound like an army. Nothing is okay.

I haven't had a nightmare like that in a long time, and I guess I forgot all the good ways to calm myself down, because nothing I try is working. I'm on my hands and knees under my covers, trying to breathe all the bad thoughts into my mattress, but nothing's working.

I need Graham.

It doesn't matter how scary he was today. I pull on an extra pair of socks because I'm shaking, and maybe it's because I'm cold.

It doesn't matter. Even when we used to fight during the day, he would always let me sleep in his bed after a nightmare. He was always nice after a nightmare. Always. He turns into a different Graham when he knows that I need him.

I pad across the hallway to his room and crack his door open. "Graham?"

For some reason, I'm terrified he won't be here. That the real nightmare was that he ever came back at all.

But he's there, of course. He cracks one eye open as I come inside. "Wil?" he says.

I nod.

"I can't see you. It's too dark."

I come up to the side of the bed. I don't know why

I'm taking all these tiny steps. His carpet is scratchy through my socks.

"Are you crying?" he says.

"I had a nightmare."

"Oh. Yeah. You get those a lot."

"Not a lot anymore."

"Oh." He doesn't move. He's just lying there, looking sleepy and confused. And bored.

My stomach twists. "Can I sleep in here with you?"

"Um. Sure."

"Like I used to."

"I remember. That'll make you feel better?"

I nod hard.

"Okay. There's room."

I squish into the bed and under the covers. He scoots back toward the wall to give me more space. He says, "Do you want me to go get Mom?"

"No, don't go."

"Okay. I won't."

"Now you tell me a story."

He's quiet for a minute. "I can't think of a good one."

"You know lots of stories."

"Yeah, but I can't think of any good ones right now."

We lie there all silent. We're not touching.

"Now you rub my back," I whisper.

"Right."

"Just a little. So that we can both pretend you weren't doing it."

He rubs between my shoulder blades. It's wrong. I don't know what it is exactly, but something about the way he's doing it is all wrong. I don't feel comforted at all. My lips are shaking. I don't want to start crying again.

"You're supposed to tell me everything's okay," I whisper. I sound so whiny, but I can't help it. Can we stop playing around? I don't feel good enough to think of some stupid trick to bring him back. I need him to just say it because he's my brother and I need him.

"Everything's okay."

"And that the dreams can't be real because you're always going to be there when something bad happens."

"They're not real."

"A-and I'm never going to get stuck anywhere without you."

"But you're not the one who got stuck," he says, and he sounds so stupid and confused and I want to hit him and kick him and pull out all his hair.

"Don't you remember why it scares me?" I say.

"The time we were locked in the car."

"And now you don't like small spaces and I don't like being alone." I don't like how simple this sounds when I have to say it out loud.

"Yeah."

And hate how he sounds like he doesn't believe it.

"It's *true*," I insist.

"I know it is."

"It happened when we were kids."

"I know. I remember. But it was a long time ago. You need to grow up and get over it. Then you'll stop having nightmares."

You need to grow up.

I roll out of the bed and stand up, because I want to get away from this zombie in my brother's bed as fast as I can. He looks up at me and says, "What?"

My throat hurts so much. And then I get an idea.

I say, "I need water."

"Okay."

"You're supposed to come with me."

He looks so tired that I expect him to groan when he gets out of bed and starts down the hall. But of course he doesn't. Why would he care that he's tired? What does tired even mean to him? What does anything mean to him?

If anything will have any meaning for him, it's this. This is the last test.

When he's in the bathroom filling up a glass of water, I slam the door on him. I push myself against it, hard, and I hold the knob so he can't open it.

"Wil?" He knocks on the door.

I realize I'm counting seconds in my head.

I'll give him thirty seconds to freak out. He will. I know him. I used to trap him in closets to torture him when I was really, really mean or really mad, and he never lasted more than five or ten seconds before falling completely apart. Screaming, crying, cursing, falling apart. It's coming. Tonight I'm giving him thirty seconds.

"Wil." He keeps knocking in this quiet, patient rhythm. "I have your water, okay? Open the door and let me out."

Twenty more seconds.

"Wil, come on. What are you doing? Open the door. Aren't you thirsty?"

Ten more seconds.

"It's kind of cold in here, Wil."

Five.

"Come on, man, this is just stupid."

Two.

One.

I open the door.

"There you go. Here." He hands me the glass of water. "What were you just doing?" He looks down at me, both his feet planted on the floor, his eyes round and calm and quiet.

He's not scared.

He's not mad at me for locking him in there. He's not trying to hurt me by pretending he doesn't care. He's just . . . not.

"I've got to go," I whisper. I walk back to my room as fast as I can. I drop the water glass, and Graham says my name, but I don't slow down.

I sit on my bed and wrap my arms around my knees and hide my face.

I'm giving up.

Three years ago, I had an ear infection and couldn't really hear anything from my left side, and my head was throbbing like I'd been trying to hold my breath for a long time. Graham made sure I was lying with my right ear up, then he told me this big, long story. He used action figures for props.

"So once the zookeeper realized it was the monkeys who stole the bananas, he knew there was only one way he'd be able to get them back."

"How?" I whispered. My throat was so sore.

"Don't talk. He had to beat them in shuffleboard, of course."

"What?"

"I said don't talk. Monkeys love shuffleboard."

He used a page from a homework assignment he'd failed and a stack of quarters to make a shuffleboard court. I watched the monkeys and the zookeeper have their showdown while I sipped the last of my apple juice.

"Need more?" Graham asked me without looking up, when my straw skidded against the dry bottom of the box.

"Uh uh."

"You're supposed to drink juice."

"I just drank some."

"More, though."

I shook my head.

"Drink more juice or the monkeys are going to kill

you. The only thing they love more than shuffleboard is beating up dehydrated sick boys."

I still pouted, but I took the new juice box when Graham forced it at me. And it wasn't so bad. And then he let me pick if I wanted to be on the side of the zookeeper or the monkeys.

Then he let me win.

I LEAVE MY ROOM early in the morning and grab a box of cereal and a bunch of juice boxes. I plunk them down on my nightstand, lock the door, and move a stack of my favorite books from the shelf to the foot of my bed.

There. I'm never getting out of bed again.

I watched this show one time about people who had to survive in the wild without food. Some of them lasted a few weeks. I have cereal, so I bet I can go way longer. Maybe Zombie-Graham will die in a heap by then, and all of this will go away and we can pretend it never happened. And I can remember the real Graham instead of this thing walking around in his body.

I'm trying to read, but thoughts keep ramming their way into my head.

What if my mom yells at Graham to do the dishes, and he gets mad and goes crazy and kills her?

What if there are zombies on the streets right now, eating people's brains?

My parents come to the door and tell me Anthony's on the phone. I don't want to talk to him. He's either going to yell at me for ripping up the notebook or tell me that his grandmother broke into the house and tried to eat everybody, and either way I don't want to hear it.

What if Anthony was right, and I made the biggest mistake of my life? What if I woke up creatures that want to kill us?

I cover my head with my pillow when my parents turn on the TV in the living room.

I don't want to know.

I guess my parents agreed to give me one day of moping, but the next day they're up bright and early, banging on my door. "The weather's so nice," Mom says.

Of course the weather's nice. It's summer. It's not like we should be celebrating that it's sunny or something.

"Get up," she says. "Dad's making pancakes."

"I don't want to," I say.

Graham hates pancakes. I say, "I'm not hungry." I'm so hungry. And if I eat any more of this cereal, I'm going to puke.

"When was the last time you saw Anthony?"

"I want to be alone."

Even Graham stops by once or twice to see if I'm okay, probably because someone makes him. I don't ask, and I don't open the door for him.

When I'm calm, I don't really think he's going to hurt me, not unless I go yelling at him for dying again. But that's not the problem. The problem is that this is all because of me, I did this, and now it's like he's dead all over again, except this time nobody cares but me.

I finally come out of my room because I don't know what else to do.

I don't know how Mom and Dad can look at him or pretend that everything's okay. They're not really any happier. They're not doing any of the things they did when they were really happy, before he died the first time. They're just walking around with these big smiles stuck on their faces. If Mom were happy, she'd be poring over her seating charts for her new class, smiling to herself as she rearranges seats like she's playing the world's best game of musical chairs. Dad would be browsing the web for more floor plans and patterns for building those miniature cities in the garage that make him so happy. I know what my parents are like when they're happy, and it isn't this. This is just fake. This is like . . . Zombie Tag.

The news is on in the living room all the time now. I try to avoid it all I can, but I let my guard down when I realize people aren't talking about zombies all the time anymore. The allure has worn off. The actress from *Tornadoes of Doom* just had a baby and no one even knew she was pregnant. This is crazy, humongous, life-changing news apparently. More interesting than zombies. I kind of agree.

Graham's learned to fake a smile and a laugh. "I look kind of normal, don't I?" he says, looking at himself in the mirror of our bathroom while I brush my teeth.

I spit.

The next morning, the news explodes with zombies again. One went crazy and started screaming at a cop or something, got kind of violent. I see stills of this girl, her hair messy and big around her head, her screaming mouth so wide it's taking up her entire face. She bit a cop, and it's big news that he didn't turn into a zombie. Sometimes I'm stunned by how stupid people are. I figured that out like five minutes after Graham woke up.

Also, they shot her and she didn't die, and apparently I'm the only one who assumed zombies were invincible after Graham's non-bleeding at the doctor, because now everyone's freaking out about that. I guess we can stop bugging Graham about taking his meds, since it's not like he cares if he feels out of breath anyway. I want to go back to bed.

Dad says if I don't get out of the house, he's going to send me to the doctor. "I'm not sick," I say.

"Then cut it out."

So I find things to do by myself. I go to the creek and scratch in the mud with a stick. I sit outside the school and play with the broken pieces of the bell. I'm really careful with them, and I keep counting them over and over to make sure I haven't lost any. I don't know why.

Stella calls. Anthony calls. Whatever. I don't answer. I've been blowing them off so long that if they weren't mad at me already, they definitely are now, so I don't have any choice but to keep blowing them off.

I don't remember how I got by all those months without Graham. It feels totally impossible to wake up now when he's not really here. I scare myself by wishing that he'd die again.

I feel a little like Graham, because it's like I don't know how to be happy anymore.

Late that night, I hear Graham in his room. It sounds like he's crying, but that can't be right.

He's just trying to trick me.

I can't help it. After four days, I'm watching Graham again. Even though I've given up hope he's going to be real again, I'm watching everything he does and comparing it to what he would have done before. The way he eats, the way he talks, the shows he watches on TV. And I get some kind of sick pleasure out of being angry at him whenever he does something—or doesn't do something, usually—that isn't like Graham.

I'll bother him sometimes just to get something out of him, but he doesn't take the bait as willingly as he did that time in his room, or else I'm not trying hard enough.

After dinner, Mom foists all the dishes into my arms before I can escape back to my room. She says, "Graham, help your brother with the dishes, okay?"

"Okay."

My knees are seriously about to give under this load. I lean toward the sink, so at least I'll pitch in that direction. "Why can't Graham just do all of them himself?"

"Because I said so."

"But he doesn't have anything better to do! It's not like *he* hates doing the dishes. *I* hate doing the dishes. Graham doesn't hate anything."

"Wil, quiet, or you'll do them alone."

Dad goes to the counter to put away the place mats and says, "Oh, Graham, bud, you got a letter today."

"Isn't that nice," Mom says. She always sounds like she's eighty now when she talks to Graham. Like she's his sweet little grandmother.

"Who's it from?" I ask.

Graham takes the letter. "Doesn't say."

"Maybe it's a bomb."

"Wil," Dad says, and Graham rips open the letter and reads it. I'm watching his face for a reaction, which is so stupid.

He shrugs and stuffs it into his pocket. "Are we doing this?" he asks, nodding toward the dishes. I take my spot at the sink. In the living room, Mom and Dad click on the news.

"So you guys can't die," I say to Graham. I'm washing; he's drying. "That must be cool."

"I don't want to talk about that, okay?"

The funny thing is, for someone without ninety-nine percent of his feelings, he's doing a good job of acting pretty depressed lately. Not that he's been really talkative since he's been back, but now Mom and Dad have to draw even the shortest sentences out of him. He spends all this time in his room, and whenever I see him, he looks like he's thinking really hard about something.

He jumps when I drop a dish.

I study him, "You okay?"

"I'm fine. Stop it, Wil, okay? Leave me alone."

Fine. I'll leave talking to my phony brother as a job for my phony parents. It's like there's no one left who realizes what a joke this all is. Like, are you kidding? My parents need to stop pretending this is my real brother, and the news needs to stop pretending this is the apocalypse. A few weeks ago, my friends and I could scare each other to death just thinking about zombies. This real thing is pathetic.

I'm going through my bookshelf looking for a book, and a picture falls out. It's a pencil drawing, so it's smeared now, but I can still make out what it is. Me in a suit.

God, that was ages ago.

I was probably eight or nine. We were sitting out on the driveway and I said to Graham, "Do you think I'll look like you when I grow up?"

He was drawing. "Nah, probably not."

I kicked at the ground. "Why not?"

"You'll be taller, definitely. You're practically taller than me already. Why am I so short? This sucks." He said this all in the same voice, so I could tell he didn't really care. Being short never bothered him much.

I said, "But what am I going to look like, do you think?"

Graham didn't say anything for a minute. He kept drawing, and I thought he was ignoring me. But after a while he handed me the paper he was working on. It was a picture of me, way older than Graham was then. I looked more like Dad than anybody. I was wearing a suit and I looked very serious and important.

In the picture, I was holding a big briefcase, and the edges of a few sheets of paper were sticking out by the handle. I imagined they were full of secret discoveries and inventions, and I was on my way to accept an award for revolutionizing energy conservation or saving a rain forest. Yeah, the rain forest one. Maybe they'd give me a little bit of the rain forest as a reward, and I could bring it home. And my kids could run around inside and climb up in the trees and play hide-and-seek. I'd be too old to play, but I'd watch them and smile.

Every single part of me was in that dream. I was wearing shiny shoes. I had a beard. I was just like Mr. Lohen and people took me very seriously. I could see it all in my head.

"Graham, what about you?"

"You're so stupid sometimes. I'm not growing up, remember?"

And then the whole fantasy deflated, because I realized he wouldn't be there.

I'M ON MY BED with Jack Bandit and a book about spaceships when Graham stops at my door and says, "Hey."

No way I'm looking up. Looking up shows weakness. "What?" I'm stronger than he is. I don't care about him. He's just a zombie in my house.

Graham said, "You didn't want me for anything tonight, right?"

I say, "What?" again, because we've barely talked since the nightmare, and we definitely haven't hung out. I definitely haven't wanted him for anything.

He says, "I have somewhere I need to be tonight, so I thought I should make sure you didn't have anything you wanted to do."

What does he think we're going to do, roast

marshmallows and have a heart-to-heart about our lives? "Yeah, well, that's real nice of you, bro."

"It just seemed polite."

"Whatever."

"Anyway . . . bye, Wil." He shrugs and leaves.

I don't care. I don't feel bad or anything. It's not like I hurt his feelings.

But then I hear him moving around the house, gathering stuff up. There's something weird about this. Graham hasn't gone anywhere he hasn't been dragged since he's come back. Why would he?

And what is he collecting?

He was acting weird, too. He's hiding something.

I close my book and sit up.

When I hear the door slam and the squeak of his bike wheels, I count to ten before I sneak out to my bike and start to tail him. I'm close enough that I can see him easily—he's wearing the baseball cap Dad got him from Russia, so he's easy to spot—but far enough that he can't hear my bike clicking when I switch gears.

We pass Stella's house and the mall. The scrapes on my knees burn each time I push down the pedals. I should have brought water. We're going slowly, but I can't remember the last time I biked this far.

I can't figure out where we're going. We've already passed all the places Graham used to hang out. Finally I figure out that we're along the same creek that flows by our synagogue, but I've never followed it up this far before. We get to where a small stone bridge spans the creek and Graham leaves his bike in the mud before stepping through the bushes and into the space underneath it. I linger about a hundred feet back for a while, then I leave my bike and approach on foot. I'm nervous every time a branch crunches under my shoe.

But when I get close enough, I stop worrying, because I can hear dozens of voices mumbling and overlapping and blending together. No one's being very loud, but there's so many of them that I know I could trample a whole tree and they wouldn't hear me. I duck behind a row of bushes by the shore.

There are over fifty people under that bridge, definitely. A few of them are Graham's age, and there's a handful of kids, but most of the people are older. A lot older.

He shakes hands stiffly with a few of the younger guys. No one's smiling, which strikes me as really weird. They're not making small talk.

Then I recognize one of the kids. Of course. They're all zombies.

I didn't know Graham had zombie friends. I guess that's nice. Except when did he meet them? He never leaves the house.

He shakes hand with a woman who introduces herself as Cynthia. "Thanks for the letter," he tells her.

Oh. The letter. Zombie mail. I guess that's kind of cool.

One of the older men says, "Are we ready?" and everyone quiets down to listen. They all nod.

Graham is standing near the front, his shoulders straight and even like a soldier. "What do we have?"

"I brought this." The old guy pulls a huge knife out of a sleeve on his belt.

I'm officially freaked. If I'd had a clue that this was going to happen, I would have been able to handle it, but I definitely wasn't prepared for one of them to produce a knife that's practically a sword. So I'm crouching down as far behind the bush as I can. I should have worn camouflage. What was I thinking? I'm the worst spy ever.

If I get killed here, I hope someone puts the Wake-Up bell back together and brings me back.

I think.

None of the zombies look surprised by the knife. "We

172

can try that," Graham says. "But I don't think it's going to do the trick."

"Oh yeah?"

"You saw the news. Guns didn't, why would a knife?"

The man frowns. "So what's your great idea?"

Graham takes a bottle out of his pocket. "All I could find."

Cynthia grabs it from him. "Bleach?"

"It's either that or find some nefarious use for my asthma meds. I don't have much to offer, okay? My house is pretty sanitized. I have a kid brother."

Way to make me sound like I'm five, Graham.

Wait, what's going on?

A woman with long gray hair says, "The bleach should work if anything does." She has a little girl on her hip, who's so obviously a zombie that she looks like a ghost, like she's going to drift away any second.

Cynthia says, "No, I don't like bleach. It's not practical on a large scale."

Gray Hair says, "Fine, I'll try it, and the rest of you can watch."

Another man says, "See, this is why I don't like bleach. Or that knife. We need something that'll take down a bunch at once. Some kind of bomb."

Oh my God.

"We discussed this." Cynthia shakes her head. "Too difficult to control."

They're planning their takeover.

I can't . . .

I don't . . .

Oh my God.

Graham takes back the bottle of bleach. "We won't know what happens unless someone tries it," he says. He takes the bottle and holds it up to his lips, but he doesn't drink.

I remember my mom putting the sick green man sticker on a bleach bottle when I was a kid. She said if I drank it, it would burn all the way down to my stomach and then all the way back up.

"I'm scared," he says, so quietly I almost miss it.

A few of the zombies scoff, but Cynthia says, "Yeah, just wait," to them, then puts her hand on Graham's shoulder. "That's why we need to figure this out."

They're killing us because they're *scared*? This isn't making sense. I need to figure out what's going on. Why are they testing the weapons on themselves? Why hasn't Graham killed me and Mom and Dad already?

How can I believe this for a second when that's *my brother* in front of me?

I want to run away. But I can't. My mind is keeping me frozen because my mind doesn't believe that my brother would really kill everyone. He'll back down.

But when he finally tilts the bottle and takes three huge swallows, most of my brain is going *don't do it Graham don't do it spit it out* but a part of me is whispering, *one less zombie.*

Because he's not my brother. He's a zombie. And they're going to kill everyone. And I did this. I did this. And, God, one less isn't going to matter when there are seventy of them and they've figured out the best way to kill us.

This is horrible.

Graham wipes his mouth and shrugs. "Nothing," he says.

"Immune to bleach and guns." She grabs the knife and pushes the point into the back of her hand. Nothing happens, like she's made of plastic. "And knives." She doesn't seem happy, but why would she? She's a zombie.

Now they know they can go after us with bleach, guns, and knives, and there's no risk to them.

They're ruling out our options.

This is like watching someone act out your night-mares.

Then it finally hits me that I'm staring at a bunch of heartless, invincible zombies holding at least two different weapons. I need to get out of here.

As soon as they're all distracted reading the warning label on the back of the bleach, I sprint. I run back to my bike and I'm gone as fast as I can pedal.

I can't think. I'm biking in these horrible wavy lines.

They're planning to kill us all. And there's probably a million more ways they can hurt us that we can't hurt them. And they know each other, and they're communicating.

My legs are already slow from the trip to the creek, but I don't care. If I slow down, even for a second, they're going to catch me and pull me down and eat my brains.

I'm going to die. I'm going to puke, and then I'm going to die.

Once I'm back in my room, I stare at my bug spray and my spatulas and the other patented ways Graham and I discovered to kill zombies. I strap the cans of bug spray onto my wrists with the Velcro straps I made. I snap on my helmet. I need boots, big zombie-killing ones, but I can probably borrow my dad's. He'll understand in the end.

I look at myself in the mirror.

The last time I looked like this, I was going over to Anthony's to play tag. Excited and nervous for what was supposed to be the best night of my life.

But this is real.

And this is all my fault. I thought I knew all about zombies because I made up some game. But now I don't know if a single thing I thought was true really is. About zombies. About my brother. About anything.

But I know I have to stop this. And that means I need to do more than just defend myself. I have to take down all the zombies. I have to protect Mom and Dad and Anthony and Luke and Stella and David and I'll probably end up having to save Eben, too.

Any minute, there could be gunfire, bombs, poison gas. Anything. And all the zombie gear in the world won't help us. Now that I've hit Graham on top of the head and it didn't paralyze him, I don't know where to start.

I need that notebook.

I call Anthony. "I need your help," I tell him.

"Where have you *been*?"

"Here."

"I've been trying to get in touch with you for a week, Wil, okay? What's up with you? Can you come over?"

"I can't. You have to come here."

I can't leave Mom and Dad alone with Graham. They've already left for their poker game, so they're going to be stumbling in at 3 a.m., which sounds like the perfect opportunity for Graham to marinate their brains in bleach or something.

"No, you should really come here. Seriously, Wil. You need to get away from Graham."

I need that notebook so badly I can almost feel it in my hands right now. "That's what I'm saying! Anthony, please, get over here now."

"No way. I don't want to be in the same house as someone like Graham, okay? Not again. Look." His voice gets quiet. "Can we forget about all of this and can you just . . . come over? I'll invite Stella and the guys and we can sleep in the basement with some stupid movie. Let's just . . . not think about all of this for a night."

He's talking about this world that sounds so far away.

And if he brings up his grandmother in that pitiful voice one more time, I'll scream. It's like he's traumatized from living with Zombie-Grandma for all of twenty minutes. "Anthony," I say. "I need you to come over here, and I need you to bring the notebook."

"So *that's* the only reason you want me over?"

"Anthony, please."

"Wil, look, the notebook's kind of . . ."

Oh God. He lost it. He burned it. It's gone.

But he says, "It's kind of personal."

My stomach feels cold. "Please don't tell me you're a zombie."

"Wil, what are you talking about? Of course I'm not a zombie."

Yeah, he isn't. He's way too drippy to be a zombie. Plus I've known him forever. I don't know why my mind even went there. I guess I'm on edge.

He says, "But seriously, I don't know if I'm okay with—"

"It's a matter of life and death, man!"

"I . . . I know that."

"*Then why don't you care?*"

I hear him breathe out all loud. "Okay. You can look at the notebook. But you're coming here. I mean it. I'm not letting you look at it on your own."

"I'm coming now."

"Eben's here now."

I breathe out hard.

"He's going home soon."

"I'm going to be there in half an hour. Half an hour *exactly*."

"Okay, Wil." It's like all the drippiness dripped out of him for a minute, and he actually sounds like he cares. "Okay. Listen. It's going to be okay."

Okay. This is fine. I'm going over to Anthony's, and Stella's going to come. And we'll find out how to kill the zombies. And I'll find out why Anthony's acting so weird. And I'll be ready for Graham as soon as I get home, which will be before Mom and Dad, so he won't have a chance to kill them. And nobody's brains will get eaten. And I'll save the whole world from the zombies.

I'll be a hero.

Which isn't even what I wanted to be.

I just wanted my brother back, and now I have to kill him.

After that thought hits me, I guess I lose it a little bit.

I know that I need to do this. Ever since I was a little kid, and my dad told me after a hard week of work, "Sometimes, Wil, it really is kill or be killed," I knew there would be a minute in my life where I'd have to make this kind of choice.

I just thought I'd get to wear a suit and come home to my little bit of rain forest, first, I guess.

And I'd rather it were *anyone* but Graham. Because I'm not just killing the zombie who's been living in my house the past few weeks. If he were the only thing I'd be getting rid of, that would be okay. That zombie needs to be stopped. I need to kill him. I want to kill him.

I don't want to kill my big brother.

I don't want to do it. I don't want to I don't want to I don't want to you can't make me I won't do it I have to do it and I hate everything.

A noise outside makes me jump and then shake. It's thunder. It's not a weapon. No one's dead. Just thunder.

There's nothing I can do until I get that notebook. It's not like there's anything *better* to do than crawl under my covers and throw bottles of bug spray at the walls and scream and cry, and there's nobody in the house, so you can't even prove it happened, and there's nothing else I could have done, and nothing felt right anyway.

I'm hiding under the covers and thinking about the time Graham called from summer camp. I tugged on Mom's arm for ages, trying to get her to give me the phone, and she finally finished nagging him about getting his laundry done and spending his money carefully and taking his inhaler and handed the phone to me.

Graham didn't even let me talk. He kept saying, "You would be having so much fun if you were here, Wil. You'd be having the time of your whole little life if you were here with me."

I kept trying to tell him about the cool stuff Anthony and I were doing. We'd caught a whole load of frogs down by the creek and named them and arranged them all into families, and we built a mudslide in our backyard with the garden hose and an old tarp.

He didn't care. He kept saying, "Trust me, Wil. This is way better. If you were here, you'd think all of that was so boring. Really stupid."

But Mom had said I wasn't old enough for sleepaway

camp, so it's not like it was my choice. It's not like I woke up and said, "You know what? I'd rather not go with Graham." It's just how it was. He didn't have to rub it in my face that he left me. There wasn't anything I could do.

I DON'T EVEN SAY HI to Anthony when he answers the door. "Where is it?" I say.

"In my room." He bites his lip. "Wil, are you okay?"

"I'm fine I'm fine I'm fine!" I'm already charging to his room. "They're coming after us, okay? They're coming after everyone. We need to figure out their weakness. If the zombie wrote it down before he died . . ."

Stella's already on the floor of Anthony's room, the notebook in her hands. "Hey."

"Hey." I plop down beside her on the carpet. "Anything?"

"There's so much here. What is this thing?"

"I found it with the bell. Anthony took it." I glare at him.

Stella says, "Anthony, what? You had a zombie diary and you didn't let Wil see it?"

He mumbles, "You don't get it."

"You take half." She flips to the middle of the notebook and rips a handful of pages out of the spine. Anthony groans.

I turn to him. "What is your problem?"

"That's really important to my dad. . . ."

"Your dad's *gone*."

He looks at me with his eyes narrowed, then he grunts something angry as he goes and sits on his bed. I guess that was kind of a low blow, but seriously, Anthony's losing his sidekick status by the minute. At this rate, it's going to Stella sharing the glory with me, and then how will he feel? Not to mention that Stella's mom will find out that she isn't out playing hopscotch with Mary Cavender, and we'll never get to have sleepovers with her anymore. And it'll be Anthony's fault.

I grab the pages Stella holds out and start reading.

We are starting to form tribes and alliances, but there is distrust even among them. I ate more than my share of rice yesterday. Anabelle would not stop screaming. We tried to silence her, knowing the townspeople will rise against us if we offer them the chance.

She could not be silenced.

Anthony says, "They're not going to hurt anyone. Please, Wil. Can you just trust me?"

185

"What do you know about this?"

"I've read the whole notebook," he says. "And I just found out some things that . . . Wil, you don't understand what they're . . ."

"Find anything?" I ask Stella.

She says, "They're testing things to see if they'll kill them."

I look at her. "Graham and the others were doing that. Does it say why?"

"I can't figure it out." She breathes out. "It's weird, though, right? Why are they testing weapons before they use them?"

"Because they want to make sure they don't get hurt, I guess."

She pulls her braids back in her hand. "How many weapons do they need to test before they decide we can't kill them? I don't get it. They're wasting time when they could be killing us."

"I . . . I don't know."

"It's definitely weird. There's got to be something we're not getting." She holds out a page.

Today we try guns, but they work no better than the knife against Annabelle. We are afraid to keep trying gunshots. We're afraid the noise will draw the townspeople closer.

"Afraid?" I whisper.

"What?"

I tear through the pages in my hand, looking for it to appear again, looking for anything other than apathy and anger. I finally find it. *As our fear grows, we search harder and harder for a way back to the cemetery.*

I show Stella the page. "Here."

She reads it. "Wait, what does that mean? They're trying to go back to the cemetery? Did they leave something there?"

She's missing the important part. "They're feeling fear."

Anthony says, "That's what I'm trying to tell you."

I look up at him.

He says, "Anger and fear. That's all they ever get back." He swallows. "I told you not to waste your time on Graham."

"You don't know that," Stella says. "They all died."

"They didn't . . ."

She says, "If they stuck around long enough, they might have gotten all their feelings back. Graham could still go back to normal."

I gave up too early. No. He's trying to kill us. I gave up way too late. I don't know.

"Shut up," I say. "You *don't know*."

"Yes I *do*!" he says.

"Hold on." I grab Stella. "Found something." I put her finger on the section I found and we read it together.

Something horrible happened today.

Sampson journeyed to the cemetery and found a small bell. The inscription read, "Ring 10 times for a shift."

"Oh oh oh, that's my bell."

Anthony says, "It's not *your* bell! It's my *dad's*!"

Sampson calculated that it was found in exactly the center of all our graves. We were all of us focused and still. We could feel the importance of the moment. But we had no last words.

He began to ring the bell, and at the last minute, my fear climbed and peaked.

I was too afraid to die.

I say, "They think the bell is going to kill them."

Stella says, "But it didn't work."

"How do you know?"

She holds up the notebook. "Because how would the zombie have written about it if it worked?"

I keep reading. My heart's beating so hard I think it might slip down my arm.

The bell rang, but I plugged my ears. The bodies started

to fall and I remained. Sampson collapsed as soon as he finished ringing, and I stayed, my ears tightly closed.

Oh my God.

I AM ALL ALONE.

Need to get out. Need to escape before they find out what I am. I'll spend my whole life in a government lab. Need to get out. So angry at those zombies, but I'll get out and start over.

"He's still alive," I tell Stella. "Get the last pages now." I sit for a second and try to breathe slowly enough to think. There's a zombie alive. Don't focus on that. He hasn't eaten our brains. Why hasn't he eaten our brains? Don't focus on that. There's a zombie weapon. I can kill the zombies. All I need is the bell. Focus on that. The bell is broken. Don't focus on that.

The zombies rang the bell and I don't know why.

There's still something I'm not getting.

Don't focus on that.

Stella is at the end of the notebook, staring at the page in her hand.

I say, "What?"

She holds it out to me. Her eyes are big and her mouth is small.

Angry at Anthony again.

What . . .

I whisper, "Anthony?"

Anthony is staring out the window, chewing his top lip. He has his hands in his pockets and his shoulders rounded up by his ears. He won't look at me.

Should never have come here to start a new life. Should have gone anywhere else. Furious with myself for choosing this place. I was so young and stupid to come here. I was only sixteen.

Meeting at the department today. They've found the bell. I ensured that it will be under my strict supervision. I will not reveal what I know at the risk of exposing my true identity.

I live in fear that someone will ring it.

I sleep with earplugs.

It's true. It's Mr. Lohen.

Mr. Lohen is a zombie.

I don't want to believe this, but it makes too much sense for me to pretend there could be any other explanation. Now I know why the bell was in his house. Why Mr. Lohen has a million dollars and two pretty awesome kids and is still so angry all the time. Why he ran as soon as the new zombies came back, because he didn't want to be found out.

"Anthony," Stella whispers.

He keeps staring out the window, but I hear him sniffle a little bit.

"Does your mom know?" Stella asks.

He shakes his head.

"Luke?"

Another shake. After a minute he turns to me. "So they're not going to hurt anybody, okay? Graham won't hurt you. Dad never hurt me." His voice is wet. "He got really, really mad at me, but he never hurt me. He doesn't . . . care enough to bother. Or he's too scared of being caught. Whatever. But he doesn't do it. Okay? Graham won't hurt you."

"I . . ."

I don't know.

Anthony says, "And if you kill the zombies, my dad might die too."

Does he really care if his dad dies?

I say, "Only if he's less than five miles away."

"I don't know where he is."

"Okay. Okay. Shh." I need to think.

"I've got to get home," I say. "I need to get to . . ."

I need to get rid of the bell so Graham can't die.

No. That's wrong.

I need to kill Graham. I need to put the bell back together before the zombies eat our brains. Or even if Anthony's right, I still need to put the bell back together before the zombies become an army of Mr. Lohens, yelling at their kids and from our TVs.

I need to . . .

I don't know.

Stella says, "Are you all right?"

"I don't know. Anthony?"

He shakes his head. I don't know if he's crying anymore.

Suddenly everything else fades away long enough for me to realize I am the worst friend in the entire universe. I can picture him alone in his room, reading that notebook and realizing who wrote it. Falling into pieces and having nobody to tell. And I've barely let him get a word in around my thoughts since this zombie thing began.

"What can I do?" I say. "How can I make this better?"

He swallows. "Can we all stay over at your house tonight? Maybe play Zombie Tag?"

God, Anthony, what? "That's really what you want?"

"I want to feel like things are normal."

"This is, like, the worst time ever for Zombie Tag."

He could not look more pitiful if someone were paying him. "Please?"

192

"I . . . Fine. When?"

"Nine?"

Nine. That's more than enough time for me to glue the pieces of the bell back together. By then, I can make it just a game again. It can be our celebration. I guess that's appropriate.

But it's Stella who really convinces me. She takes my hand and looks at me closely, and says, "We miss you, Wil."

I take a deep breath. "Bring the notebook, okay?"

Anthony swallows and nods. Stella grins and says, "I'll put it in my backpack."

WHEN I GET HOME, Graham isn't back yet, so I figure I can take a minute before I start putting the bell back together.

I go into his room, just to take it in. I'm staring at the walls, decorated with all the same posters I used to wonder if he'd give me when he outgrew them. I always wanted to decorate my room like his. So many times in the past few months, I wanted to peel those bikini girls off his walls and put them up on mine instead. But I knew they wouldn't be right without Graham.

Now I wish I'd taken them.

I go into my room to check on the pieces of the bell. It's only in a few pieces. I can put it back together as good as new. I know Graham could. He was always so good at puzzles.

I find a bottle of superglue in my desk and sit down. I'm about to get to work, then I hear the front door crack open. If Graham gets his hands on these pieces, it's all over. He'll flush them and eat my brains to the rhythm of the toilet tank refilling.

I stuff the pieces back into the bag and underneath my nightstand. Where's my spatula? God, where's my spatula? I find it after what feels like hours. I can't fight zombies without it. It's my zombie security blanket. And . . . honestly, it's all I have.

Graham's footsteps are getting closer and closer. Spatula. Bug spray. Okay. I fight him off, I subdue him, I disable him until I can put the bell back together. That's all I need to do. It's all I can do.

I put on my helmet and my hockey face mask and meet him in the hallway.

He stares at me. His eyes go from my caged face to my bug spray to my spatula. "Hey, Wil. Off to fight some zombies?"

I nod.

"I thought we decided bug spray was a bad idea."

I'd almost forgotten we figured all this out together.

He says, "Remember that time we played in the basement, and everything smelled like bug death for a week?"

195

I look at the spray can. "And you couldn't breathe."

"Yeah."

I lower the can. It feels like something just got drained out of me.

Or that I just realized I won't be able to do it. How am I supposed to kill him when I won't even risk fogging him with bug spray?

I failed.

I suck.

I failed humankind.

"What's up?" he says.

I don't know what else to say. "I was at your thing tonight. The zombie thing. I saw you guys."

He stays still for a long time, like he's waiting for me to admit more. But then he slowly starts to nod. "So I guess we should talk, then."

I look at him. I glue my eyes to his eyes. He doesn't try to pull away. So I say, "Are we going to talk, or are you going to hurt me?"

"We're going to talk, Wil. I promise."

I keep studying him. I'm looking for the twitch in his face, the tic that will give away that he's lying, that he's already chosen the perfect spice for my brains, but nothing gives.

I'm probably sealing my fate as zombie food, but I believe him. Because I really want to. And because if I'm really too cowardly to take him out, I guess it doesn't really matter if I'm the first victim or the last.

I take my death march into his room and sit down next to him on the bed.

He touches my arm. "Wil . . ."

"No." I pull away.

"Come on."

"I saw you, okay? You're *bad*." I hate him all over again. And I hate this room. "I don't even know you."

"Wil . . . you didn't see what you think you saw."

He wants me to look at him, I can tell, but I can't. I'm staring at my feet while I push the carpet back and forth, making the colors change a little as I push the fibers one way and then another. Right now, this little patch of carpet is my whole world.

"Are you okay?" he asks me.

"Yeah." I mumble. "I'm awesome."

"You're kind of scraped up."

I look at my arms. I guess I am. "There were brambles where I was hiding."

"You should get some Band-Aids."

I don't say anything. I don't mention that he'd already scraped me up pretty badly before the brambles.

He twists his hands in his lap. "How long were you there? You left before the smoke bomb thing, right?"

"What?"

"We were just testing it," he says.

"*You* were?" Now I'm listening to him breathe.

"I left first. That's . . . why I left." He got scared. "I knew I'd probably be fine, but . . . I didn't want to die like that again."

Not funny. Not funny. "I left way before then," I say.

"Oh. Good."

"After you drank the bleach."

"That didn't taste so good." He laughs a little in this way that doesn't sound happy or real. He rubs his forehead. "I'm glad you got out of there before we tried anything big."

I don't want to know what else they tried. "What do you even care? It's not like you like me." I don't mean like me. I mean love me. But I can't even think those words without feeling like I'm going to cry.

"Wil . . ."

"You just want us all dead! You're trying to trick

198

me into liking you again and then you're going to kill me!"

"That's not what . . . *no*, kid, listen. That's not what's going on here."

"You were testing weapons!"

He grabs both of my hands and holds them like he found them and they're important. "We were testing them on ourselves. Listen to me. We're trying to kill *ourselves*, Wil."

This hits me so hard that it feels like the world tilts.

They aren't trying to kill us. They're trying to kill themselves.

Just like the first zombies.

The bell wasn't a mistake.

Graham is trying to kill himself.

"Well, not kill." He rubs the back of his head, messing up his hair. That hits me in my stomach like a punch. He always used to do that. "Just . . . go back. We're already dead, so we can't really . . ."

"You're not dead."

"Yeah, we are."

"You're not *dead*! I *brought you back*!"

I brought them back. And it wasn't a horrible mistake. They're not bloodthirsty monsters. They're not soulless bodies. They're stiff people who feel anger and fear. They're not dead. I brought them back and they're not trying to kill us.

So they can't just leave again.

His voice is really gentle. "Wil, come on. You know I'm not the same as I was."

I hate him for being calm about this. "So you're just going to *bail*? You don't know what's going to happen. You could get all your feelings back! You can't just kill yourself because you're *bored*."

He clenches his hands and lets them go immediately. "It's not because we're bored. I don't know bored."

"I hate you."

"We're going to die anyway, no matter what we do. The other zombies died. We know it's possible."

"That doesn't mean you have to go looking for how to do it!"

"It means it's—look at me, Wil—it means it's inevitable. That's what we know. It's all we know."

"Why is it inevitable?" I whisper.

He pauses. "We know that we're going to die. It's going to happen. Even if we try to live for as long as we can, we're going to die."

"*Everyone's* going to die." But that doesn't mean I want to think about it.

"But you don't know what it's going to be like," Graham tells me.

"You could be normal again!"

"Yeah. I could be normal again." He says this like it's the worst thing he's ever heard.

And I want to shake him. "You could be *real*. You don't know what could happen. You could turn normal again. Maybe it just takes *time*."

"You don't understand. I can't . . . be normal again."

"Why *not*!"

"Because I can't go through that again!"

He's breathing hard. His shoulders are heaving. I think he's expecting me to talk, but I have no idea what to say.

He doesn't want to have feelings, and here he is falling apart in front of me more than he ever has.

Maybe he's going to hit me again.

I touch his knee and he jerks his leg away.

I say, "You're supposed to have feelings. That's what kids have. Like, real, living kids." I want to prove this with props or drawings. I want to make it real the same way he made those stupid stories real for me.

"Then why did I lose them?" he says.

I shift so I'm facing him. His bed creaks underneath me like I weigh a million pounds. "Because you weren't alive. But . . . Graham, you can come back now. You're here."

He rubs his forehead with both hands. "And what about when my zombie body gives out or someone figures out whatever it was that killed us last time and kills all of us? What if I find out that being invincible means weapons can't hurt me but I can still have a heart attack or fall and hit my head or . . ." He gestures toward his chest, then takes a deep breath. "In a month or five years or a hundred years I'm going to die again. I'm going to have to go through it just like I did before. With all the feelings. And it's going to hurt." He puts his head in his hands. "It hurts so much."

"But you get five or fifty or a hundred years first." And dying takes, like, ten minutes, tops.

I don't get it. How can he be so afraid of dying when he's already done it once?

"It's too hard." He shakes his head. "I don't want to die again."

"Wait, *what*? If you're so scared of dying, why are you all trying to die?"

He breathes out and speaks slowly. "If I go back now, go back to being dead . . . I only have a few feelings now. Dying isn't going to be that bad. I'll forget it all really soon. It won't hurt too much. I'm practically dead already."

"You're not making any sense." I sound like a little kid, which just makes me angrier.

He looks at me, and his eyes are so big and brown. He looks really young. "Dying now would be easy, Wil. Going now. It's easy and it doesn't hurt."

"It hurts *me*!" I kick his leg. It's so stupid, but I need to hurt him right now. I need to just do whatever I can to hurt him a little bit. "We went through all of this so I could have my brother back again, and you're just going to ruin that?"

"No. Listen to me. You *can't* have your brother back. You can't."

"You're just saying that to be mean because you don't have any feelings!"

He gives me that look, the one I hate. The one when he acts like he's so much smarter than I am. "And what does that tell you, huh? Didn't your brother have feelings?"

"You're Graham. You're right here."

"Yeah, but I'm not . . . I'm never going to be the same. You know that. Your brother died in that bathroom."

"Shut up." *Don't you ever say that.*

"You know it's true, Wil."

No, I don't. "You could try. You don't know for sure. You could get feelings back if you stuck around. You *don't know*."

"Which is why I need to do this now. Before they have a chance to come back."

I hate him. I hate him. I don't even know why I want him to be alive. "You're a coward. What about Mom and Dad?"

"They'll deal. You know they'll deal."

I know it and I hate it. "What about *me*?"

"I have to do this, Wil. I need to get it over with now so I don't have to feel every single thing I've had stripped away from me and replaced with empty instead. I'm not going to do that again." He swallows. "No one should have to do that twice."

"No."

"Do you think dying in that bathroom was *comfortable*, Wil? Do you think it was *fair*?"

No. But I think it meant something.

I think it came with feelings.

"Why are you telling me all this?" I whisper.

"Because you thought I was going to eat your brains, yeah?" He plays with my spatula. "This thing probably wouldn't have helped you much, you know? You think we're immune to bleach but not cooking tools?"

I yank my spatula away.

He says. "I need you to stay out of this. No more tagging along to meetings. We have a lot more stuff to test, and I don't want you to get hurt."

"You don't care if I get hurt."

He exhales.

"You don't care if I get hurt, and you don't even want to die! You don't want anything. You don't *have any feelings*!" I push myself off the bed. "You don't know *how* to want *anything*!"

"Wil. Please. I'm scared. I'm so scared."

"You don't know what scared means! Do you know how scared *I've* been? You're some stupid imitation of scared, and you want to die before you have to feel the real thing!"

"The scared is real." His eyes are big and his breathing is speeding up. "Seriously, trust me, the scared is real."

"*Your scared is stupid and fake just like you!* And you know what?" I spin around and face him. "I worry about dying. Everyone worries about dying. When I can't sleep, I spend the whole night scared I'm going to die and everyone's going to forget about me. And the world *won't* stop."

I see him swallow and remember.

I say, "And then it's morning and I get over it and I go to school or I go play, because only grownups and *cowards* are allowed to shut down and be scared of dying. And you're a *coward*."

"Or a grownup," Graham whispers.

I feel like he's thrown a bucket of ice water on me.

Eventually, I say, "Even worse."

We don't say anything.

I hate that he looks the same as he always has.

I say, "Anyway, everything you said is stupid, because you guys never even figured out how the other zombies killed themselves, so you're just going to live forever and be angry and I'm going to be angry at you."

I think maybe I gave away that I know more than he does, because his face seems to narrow a little as he studies me. "No," he says after a minute. "We don't know how."

But it doesn't matter if he knows. Because in a minute, I'm going to trash the bell and he'll be here forever. He'll be this coward and this jerk and he'll be in front of me forever and ever until he gets real again and he is sorry and he apologizes for the rest of our really long lives.

Then the doorbell rings.

EBEN'S GOING, "I want to be Zombie God. I never get to be Zombie God. Come on, Wil, it's totally my turn. Come on, give me the pen, Wil, it's my turn."

"Oh my God, fine. Here. I don't care." I'm not sure anyone has ever been as clueless as Eben, ever.

I hand him the pen and the Post-its and go over to Stella. She's in the corner talking to Anthony, who looks like he's recovering from a bad case of the flu, which is better than he's looked in weeks, really. "How are you?" I ask him. Then I give him a quick hug, since no one's watching but Stella, and I know she won't laugh because she touches everyone all the time.

He shrugs.

I don't know what to say. Even telling him that I'm not going to let the zombies kill themselves isn't going to make him feel any better about having the world's worst father. So I just say what he told me. "It's going to be okay."

He nods like he believes me, which is kind of heartbreaking, actually.

Then I say, "I hope you get to be Zombie," which is kind of funny, considering all that's happened, and he smiles.

David calls, "Hey, guys, are we playing?"

The three of us rejoin David and Eben and grab our Post-it Notes. Anthony darts his flashlight around, checking all the corners of my basement.

"Graham's upstairs," I whisper to him.

"I know." He swallows. "I'm not scared of Graham."

"I know you're not." I peek at my Post-it and shove it into my pocket. Not zombie. I look at Stella and decide to risk that she isn't either. I whisper, "After this, come with me."

She looks at me and nods.

We close our eyes and stomp our feet so the zombie can sneak out of the circle to hide the dinosaur bank. I feel a little puff of air next to me, and I smile a little. It's Anthony.

Good for him.

Once he's tapped us each on the shoulder, we open our eyes and grab our spatulas. "Didn't hear anyone go up the stairs," Eben says, swinging his flashlight between each of us. "So I'll be checking down here."

"Knock yourself out, Eben." I catch Stella's eye and jerk my head toward the stairs. She nods, and she's right beside me all the way to my room.

"What are we doing?" she whispers.

"You have the notebook?"

She holds it up.

"We're destroying it. And the bell."

"*What?*"

"I'll explain later. Just trust me, okay?" I flop down on my stomach and squirm under my nightstand until I feel the baggie between my fingers. I pull it out. The pieces of the bell click against each other. "Come on. Bathroom."

She follows me to the bathroom and sticks her BAR-RICADE Post-it on the wall before she closes the door.

"Tell me what's going on," she says.

"They're not trying to kill us. They're trying to kill themselves, and the only way they can do it is with this bell. I get rid of the bell, I save Graham."

"They're not going to hurt us?"

"They're not. I promise. Remember what Anthony said? His dad's never hurt him. They're too *scared* to try to hurt us."

"You're sure about this?"

"Positive."

I hear Eben screaming. I guess staying in the basement didn't work out that well for him after all. Heh.

There are footsteps in the hall, and Stella and I hold our breath. But no one starts pounding at our door.

"Do it," she says. "If you're sure, do it. Hurry."

I hold the baggie over the toilet.

Drop, flush, and it's over. That's all it takes. If I do that, he's here forever.

Zombie Graham is here forever.

She says, "Wil, hurry up, come on!"

Graham, who doesn't feel anything and never will.

I grab the sink to keep myself steady and put the baggie on top of the medicine cabinet. "Give me the notebook."

"Why?"

"Please?"

She does. I open the cover and take out all the pages we've stuffed back in. They're all out of order, but it doesn't matter. They all say the same thing. The whole book is the same thing over and over, because zombies don't change. They don't.

I keep tearing through the notebook anyway, looking for anything, some shred of hope that Graham can possibly be who he was again. Anything. There has to be some way that he can come back.

But every single entry is the same. Angry. Mad. Frustrated. Scared. Terrified. Angry again. There's nothing else. There are no other feelings. Mr. Lohen started this journal thirty years ago, and since then he's been nothing else.

These zombies are nothing but angry and scared.

And I can't lie to myself and tell me there's hope of being something more, because I've seen Mr. Lohen. He's not any happier than the kid who wrote these entries thirty years ago.

"But he's still alive," I whisper.

Stella touches my elbow. "Wil?"

"He's still alive. And being alive doesn't hurt him." Either I'm shaking or her hand is. "Stella . . . it doesn't hurt him to stay alive, because hurting is a feeling, and he doesn't have feelings, so if he can stay alive for me, then he should. He should. I can make him stay alive for me and that isn't bad because it doesn't hurt him to be alive."

"But he has the bad feelings. He's mad and he's scared."

"They're not real. They're zombie feelings."

"You've seen Mr. Lohen scream."

"That hurts us. It doesn't hurt him."

She says, "But the fear—"

Our sentences are overlapping and we're breathing fast and everything is slamming together in my brain and I don't know what to do.

Then something crashes on the stairs, and Anthony's voice rings from down the hallway. "Braaaaaaaaaains!"

Stella looks at me. Her eyes are huge and getting bigger.

"We've got to go," I say.

"Fast."

"Braaaaaaaaaains!" David screams, and I think I hear Eben, too. It's just us.

"I'll investigate," Stella says. She creeps out the bathroom door, but she's back in a second. "They're looking for us in the living room. We've got to make a break for it. If they catch us in here, they'll bang down the door and we're zombie food."

"Okay." I look at the baggie in my hand.

"Wil, if you're going to do it, do it now."

"I . . . I don't know." I can't decide. I need more time.

"BRAAAAAAINS!" someone screams. My heart's pounding like it's switching gears every few beats.

"I'll figure it out later." I leave the notebook on top of the toilet, stuff the baggie in my pocket, and grab Stella's hand on our way out the door.

Graham's out in the hallway. He looks confused and a little jumpy. Maybe the noise woke him up. I glance down at my pocket to make sure none of the bell is hanging out. Safe.

"Go back to your room!" I whisper at him. "You didn't see us."

"Why's everyone yelling?"

"We're *playing*! Go back to your room!"

Stella tugs me, and I give Graham one more stern look before Stella and I dart to my room, where at least there are more places to hide if they break in. I put my Post-it on the door.

I haven't turned on the light, so all I can see is the carpet by the door that's lit from the hall, and some of my bedspread and half of one of my posters by the window.

The zombies have quieted down, and all I can hear is Stella breathing.

"I guess we should look for the Key," she says.

"Um . . . yeah."

But neither of us moves. For a minute there, the game felt really important, like it used to. But now it's faded into the back again. But this time, instead of thinking about Graham and how scared I am, I'm thinking about Stella, and how heavy and alive my dark room feels.

"I always thought the real thing would be like this," she whispers.

"What?"

"Zombies."

"Me too, really."

Now that I'm adjusting to the dark, I can see her outline and the way her grip chokes up on her spatula. "I guess things aren't always how you imagine them," she says.

Then I lean over and kiss her cheek, before either of us can think about it anymore. Her skin is really warm, like there's electricity down in her bones.

She turns her head toward me, but neither of us says anything. Somehow, that feels perfect for right now.

Then she whispers, "Thanks," and that feels even better.

The pounding on the door starts, and we both jump,

but it isn't our door. The zombies are down the hall, trying to break down the abandoned barricade for the bathroom.

"They think we're still in there," I say.

We peek out my bedroom door. There they are, hitting the door with their fists and crying out for brains.

I have that sick feeling in my stomach again, just like every time we end up trying to get into the bathroom. My head's starting to cloud a little—*we have to get it, my brother's in there, I have to save them.* But this time, I know it isn't real. I guess my days of fantasy-saving Graham are over.

Then I hear something. The zombies are chanting in unison, but when they pause to take a breath, someone is still screaming.

Stella looks at me. She hears it too. *Graham?* she mouths.

Graham.

I run out into the hallway and put one hand on Anthony's shoulder and one on David's. "Guys. Stop."

"*BRAAAAAINS!*" Eben roars, while he lunges at me.

"I said *stop!*" I swing my spatula at him and he backs off. "I'm not kidding. Game over."

Graham is still screaming. It's definitely coming from

inside the bathroom. He's really in there. Why is he screaming?

"You can't just call game over," David says.

"Shut up. Yes, I can. Graham?" I try the doorknob, but it's locked. "Graham, are you in there?"

He is. I can hear him. He's crying. He's wheezing.

"Graham, *let me in*!"

Then his voice, heavy like it always is when he cries, just like mine. "I can't get out."

"Yes you can!" I grab the knob again. "Unlock the door!"

"I—"

"*Unlock it you can do it!*"

There's a little more fumbling, then the lock clicks open. David whispers, "Is he okay?"

"Stay out here," I tell all of them, and I slip into the bathroom.

Graham is standing by the shower, his arms around himself. All the notebook pages are on the floor around him, except for the one in his hand. The one about the bell. He found that fast.

But right now, I can tell it means nothing to him. The only thought in his head is that he was trapped. That he almost died.

That he did die once.

"I thought I was stuck. I thought that I couldn't get out and that no one was going to get in in time. I'm so stupid."

"You're not stupid. You were scared."

Not fake, washed-out, unimportant scared.

Really, horribly scared.

He puts his hands on his knees to breathe, still choking out sobs between breaths. "God. Oh my God. Oh my God."

This is the only thing he's ever going to be, when he's not so angry he could explode. These are his choices.

Those are the only choices he has if he tries to stay alive when he isn't supposed to. He isn't supposed to stay here.

He has to go back.

And me . . . my only choices are, either Graham's going to be sad forever, or I'm going to be sad forever without him.

But I can be other things besides sad, and he can't. That's the difference. I can bounce back. I am strong and invincible and brave.

And he's not anymore.

"Come here," I say, and I hold him. His whole body sags into me, but I know it's only because he's tired. I know comforting him isn't going to do anything, but I'm doing it anyway. Because this is how I'm going to say goodbye this time.

I take the baggie from my pocket and slip it into his hand. "Everything's going to be okay," I whisper.

While my friends sleep downstairs, Graham and I sit in his room and glue the bell back together. Well, I glue. He draws and trusts me to do a good job.

Everything feels almost normal. I tell him a joke, one of my best ones, just to see if he laughs. He doesn't. I had to be sure.

So I guess the bottom line is, dead people don't really come back.

And I'm dealing with that.

Sucks.

I finish gluing the bell back together, and I trade it to him for the picture he drew. It's me, sitting on his shoulders. I can't remember the last time we did that. I'm too big for it now. I'd crush him.

"I should probably get going," he says. "We want to make sure we all go together."

I nod and swallow.

"Hey," he says. "You're going to be fine."

"I know." Before I can think if I mean it, I say, "Can I come with you?"

He answers just as quickly, "No. No way." And then he hugs me. When I expect him to give up and pull away, he doesn't.

I let my cheek fall onto his shoulder. He feels so solid and so cold. "But why not?"

"Because I'm your big brother and I said so. You stay here. Be big."

Be big. That's the last thing Graham says to me.

For real this time.

Bye.

WHEN I WAKE UP, it's over.

At breakfast, it's me and Mom and Dad, sitting just the three of us at the kitchen table. The television's in the background, announcing what the police came and told us a few hours ago: that the zombies were all found dead, lying on top of their graves. Mom and Dad were trying to decide whether we were going to have another funeral, but they weren't looking at each other and their voices were so quiet. And now nobody's saying anything. They decided they didn't want another funeral. I don't think we know what the next thing is to say.

So I say, "What do we do now?" Just to say something. Just so they'll look at me.

Mom stops peeling her orange. She looks at me. She sees me.

"Now we keep going," she says. She goes to the sink and washes the orange peel off her hands. Then she hugs me. She is warm and real. Dad sits next to me and puts one hand on my shoulder and one on Mom's, and we sit like that together for a long time.

I don't cry, but I have this feeling that it would be fine if I did, and that's more of a relief than I can even describe.

But God, I'm sick of crying.

I'm sure Anthony's going to hate me forever, but when I call, he says, "You know? I'm sort of glad my grandmother's gone. She was really a stick in the mud."

"Yeah."

"I talked to Stella. You did the right thing, you know? For Graham."

"I hope so."

"Me, too."

"What about your dad?" I say.

"We're okay without him. Luke's even mowed the lawn yesterday." There's a long pause, then he says, "I think Dad was smart enough to know to stay five miles away, don't you?"

"Yeah. Yeah, definitely." I clear my throat. "But if he shows up and starts eating someone's brains, we're totally on to him."

"Totally." Then he quickly says, "Do you want to come over tonight?"

I guess we both know there's a possibility that I let Graham take out Mr. Lohen along with the rest of the zombies, but I also know that it's Anthony's choice whether he wants to worry about it. And I don't think he does. I think he wants to move on.

I'm pretty amazed by my drippy best friend, to be honest.

I say, "My parents did tell me I should go do something fun. Which is weird."

"Yeah, I want to do something fun. Luke keeps blowing me off."

"Yeah?"

"I just asked him about this video game, and he told me he was too busy and he didn't care."

It was like something loosened in my chest. "Yeah, I'll come over. I'll totally come over. You can tell me all about Luke."

"Good. Come back to us, okay?"

I don't understand exactly what he means, but I get it well enough to say, "I will," and really mean it.

Three hours later, we're all in Anthony's basement with our flashlights and spatulas. I open my Post-it Note and peek at it. BARRICADE. That's okay. I didn't want to be the Zombie tonight. And I can tell by the look on Stella's face that she got it. It's about time.

"Want to hunt together?" I ask Anthony.

"Totally. But don't be surprised if it turns out I have to eat your brains."

We sprint to the downstairs bathroom and tear it apart for the toy yeti we're using as the Key. "So," Anthony says, really casually. "Are you okay?"

"I don't know."

"Well . . . you know. I'm here. If you want to talk."

I say, "I will. But right now I just want to play."

"Well, the Key's not in here, so we better hurry up or we're just going to *die*."

"Okay, come on. Kitchen!"

I run up the stairs with Anthony. As we're rooting through the cabinets, I realize that I'm smiling. Which is weird, because I'm really into the game right now, and dying of a zombie bite is no laughing matter. So there's no good reason I should be smiling.

Though I guess if I have to die by a zombie bite, I hope it's Stella doing the biting.

Someone screams from the second floor. Anthony grabs my arm.

"Oh no. Okay. Check the living room!"

While Anthony makes a break for the living room, I duck down the hallway. I don't know why, but it's like there's a voice in my ear telling me to check the laundry room. Like the real Zombie God is looking down on me and telling me how to find the Key to get out of this house.

I'm almost there when Stella, in full Zombie mode, jumps out of the guest room and lands in front of me. "*I want your brains!*" she shouts. She always gets really hyperactive when she's a zombie. It's terrifying.

I hit her on top of her head to paralyze her, and she immediately drops to the floor. She's still twitching a little, but I guess we can count that as paralysis.

I'm glad that still works.

I jump over her and slam my BARRICADE Post-it Note on the door of the laundry room. Almost immediately, she's banging on it. And she has at least one other set of fists with her. Our population is dwindling!

Thirty seconds. I check all the shelves, but I don't find anything. I open the washing machine and tear through the wet clothes. This is really gross.

For some reason, I'm convinced that if I find the Key, everything really is going to be okay. This is what will do it, finding this stupid yeti doll. I can't believe this is what it's come down to, but I'm not going to be the one to argue with the universe anymore. Yeti doll or bust.

And it's so stupid that I think that will make everything okay, because right now I don't even know what "everything" is. Not to mention "okay."

Underneath a soaked pair of jeans, I find a damp stuffed yeti.

Yes!

I open the door as fast as I can and I run. David and Anthony and Stella and Eben are all at my doorway, arms outstretched, mouths craving my brains, but I fight through them with my spatula. I'm unstoppable. I'm going to win. I have this. I invented this game. Me and Graham invented this game.

"I have the Key!" I yell as I run past. "I have the Key, I have the Key!" They're chasing me down, right on my heels, because they don't want me to win, but there's nothing they can do about it, because I can leave the house. I can get out. The front door is right in front of me. I can hear Anthony breaking character and cheering for me.

I rip the door open and run onto the front porch. The air is heavy and hot and dark and I breathe it as long and as hard as I possibly can.

I'm alive. I'm alive I'm alive I'm alive I'm alive I'm alive.

ZOMBIE TAG
RULES

NUMBER OF PLAYERS: at least 4

OBJECTIVE: If you are a zombie, turn everyone else into a zombie. If you are a human, escape the house.

- One person is Zombie God. This is a great honor, usually granted to you if it is 1. your birthday or 2. your house.

- The Zombie God has one very important job. He writes ZOMBIE on one Post-it Note and BARRI-CADE on the remaining Post-it Notes. He shuffles the notes and passes one to each player, keeping one for himself. The Post-its are secret and none of the players, including the Zombie God, know what Post-its the others have. The Zombie God's job is now over.

● Everyone secretly looks at their Post-it Notes. Chances are you are a human, in which case your Post-it will say BARRICADE. But it might say ZOMBIE. No matter what, keep that note and keep your face neutral.

● Everyone gathers in a circle and closes their eyes. At this point, the lucky player with the ZOMBIE Post-it sneaks out of the circle. In some versions of the game, all players will stomp their feet to drown out the sound of the sneaking. But true zombies will not need this as they move silently and possibly with the power of invisibility.

● The Zombie takes a predetermined object—preferably a toy, a doll, or someone's little sister—and hides it somewhere in the house. This object is the Key. You need to find it in order to escape the house.

● After hiding the Key, the Zombie returns and runs around the circle, tapping each person on the head. Once you are tapped on the head, you silently count to ten before opening your eyes. This allows the Zombie to sneak back into the circle unnoticed.

● It is now time to play. Grab a flashlight and a spatula. You will need them.

● You may either strike out on your own or team up with as many people as you like to search the house for the Key. The Zombie, at this point, pretends to search as well.

● The Zombie has thirty seconds to pretend to be normal. When the thirty seconds are up, he reveals himself as the Zombie ("RAWWWR, BRAINS," etc.) and attempts to bite as many humans as possible. Ears are a good target, but anywhere will do. Bite gently, because zombies have weak teeth that might fall out with too much force.

● If you are the victim of an attempted zombie attack, you have four ways to escape:

1. Fight him off with your spatula. Zombies are terrified of spatulas.

2. Hit him on the top of his head with the flat of your hand (again, gently, so his teeth don't fall out. A toothless zombie is a terrifying opponent). This is the zombie paralysis move that will freeze the Zombie for ten seconds, allowing you to make an escape.

3. Run. Be warned, however: Zombies possess super speed.

4. Slap your BARRICADE Post-it on a door, close it, and hide in that room. The Zombie, upon encountering a barricaded door, must bang on it for thirty seconds to break the barricade before he can enter. This should give you time to find the Key if it is hidden in this room. If you find the Key you will need to find an alternate route out of the room or fight the Zombie long enough to sprint to the front door. Or, if the Key is not in the room, it is enough time for you to call your mother and tell her you love her.

- If you are bitten you become a zombie. But all is not lost! You now begin hunting the others with your zombie compatriots.

- If you are a human and you find the Key, run toward the front door. If you escape, you win! You are now the only hope for humanity.

ACKNOWLEDGMENTS

As always, thanks to my fabulous agent, Suzie Townsend, and everyone at FinePrint. A million pounds of gratitude to my incredible editor, Nancy Mercado, and the entire team at Roaring Brook for their trust in this story and in the value of a good spatula.

Thanks to my creative writing teacher, Tom Earles, who said he wanted to write a zombie book after he wrote his "real novel," and Dr. David Wyatt, who believed me when I told him my zombie book was my real novel. And to everyone who supports me, day in and out: Mom, Dad, Abby, Alex, Seth, Christopher, and the Musers. There is no one like you.